Nothing could have prepared Ethan for the need that took over his body.

In that moment he captured her mouth with a desperate possession that fueled his fire as it had never been fueled before. He wanted to devour her alive.

A part of him couldn't believe that she was in his arms and that he was enveloping her mouth as if it were the only one left on earth, which for now, for him, it was.

He couldn't control the rush of physical hunger consuming his entire being. His tongue tangled with hers with a voracity that sent pleasure spiking throughout both of their bodies. He was kissing her with hunger, as if he were seeking out some forbidden treat that he was determined to find.

Moments later, only because they needed to breathe, he released her mouth and stared into her stunned gaze. Refusing to allow her time to think again, he lowered his mouth once more and at the same time swept her off her feet and into his arms. Before the night was over, his touch would be imprinted on every inch of her skin.

Books by Brenda Jackson

Kimani Romance

*Solid Soul
*Night Heat
*Beyond Temptation
*Risky Pleasures
In Bed with the Boss
*Irresistible Forces
Just Deserts
The Object of His Protection
Temperatures Rising
*Intimate Seduction
Bachelor Untamed
*Hidden Pleasures
Star of His Heart

*Steele Family titles
**Westmoreland Family titles

Kimani Arabesque
(all Madaris Family titles)

Tonight and Forever
A Valentine's Kiss
Whispered Promises
Eternally Yours
One Special Moment
Fire and Desire
Something to Celebrate
Secret Love
True Love
Surrender
**Wrapped in Pleasure
**Ravished by Desire
Sensual Confessions

BRENDA JACKSON

is a die "heart" romantic who married her childhood sweet-heart and still proudly wears the "going steady" ring he gave her when she was fifteen. Because she's always believed in the power of love, Brenda's stories always have happy endings. In her real-life love story, Brenda and her husband of thirty-six years live in Jacksonville, Florida, and have two sons.

A *New York Times* bestselling author of more than fifty romance titles, Brenda is a recent retiree who worked thirty-seven years in management at a major insurance company. She divides her time between family, writing and traveling with Gerald. You may write Brenda at P.O. Box 28267, Jacksonville, Florida 32226, by e-mail at WriterBJackson@aol.com or visit her Web site at www.brendajackson.net.

BRENDA JACKSON

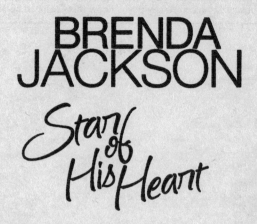

Star of His Heart

KIMANI
ROMANCE

KIMANI PRESS™

ISBN-13: 978-0-373-86172-9

Recycling programs
for this product may
not exist in your area.

STAR OF HIS HEART

Dear Reader,

I enjoy doing continuity books where I get to work with other authors. This particular continuity, Love In the Limelight, is special in that I get to work with three authors whose work I admire and enjoy reading— A.C. Arthur, Ann Christopher and Adrianne Byrd. I've even nicknamed Adrianne the "Plot Queen" because you never know where her sizzling and titillating love stories will take you.

A.C., Ann, Adrianne and I want to introduce you to the glitz and glamour of Hollywood through four beautiful women—Rachel, Charlene, Livia and Sofia. You will read about their trials, tribulations and, of course, their men. Especially their men. Being a romantic at heart I love to read a sensual romance story with a sexy hero, and I believe these four stories will more than whet everyone's romantic appetite.

So take a break, chill a moment and indulge yourself in a little romance. *Star of His Heart* tells the story of a woman who is afraid to love and the man who is determined to cure her of that fear. Every woman should have an Ethan Chambers in her life at least once.

I hope all of you enjoy reading Ethan and Rachel's story as much as I enjoyed writing it.

Happy reading!

Brenda Jackson

ACKNOWLEDGMENTS

To Gerald Jackson, Sr. You're still the one
after all these years!

To all my readers who will be joining me in April
on the Madaris/Westmoreland Cruise 2011.
Be ready to have a lot of fun!

To my Heavenly Father. How Great Thou Art.

A good name is to be chosen rather than great riches,
loving favor rather than silver and gold.
—*Proverbs* 22:1

Chapter 1

"Quiet on the set!
"Take one!
"Action!"

The director's voice blared from the bullhorn and the words sent a pleasurable thrill up Rachel Wellesley's spine. She had known before she'd uttered her first words as a child that she had an overabundance of artsy bones in her body.

The only problem was that as she got older, her choice of an artistic career would change from week to week. First she had wanted to become a painter, then a writer. Later on she had considered becoming a fashion stylist. But at the fine arts college she'd attended, after she took theory and practicum classes on beauty, she had finally decided on a career as a makeup artist and wardrobe designer. This was the life she lived for and what she enjoyed—being on the set of a movie. Or in this case, the TV set that was taping the popular prime-time medical drama *Paging the Doctor*.

It was day one of shooting for the second season. All the cast members from last season had returned except for Eric Woods, who'd played Dr. Myles Bridgestone. No one had been surprised to hear his contract was not renewed, especially with all his personal drama last season. The well-known Hollywood movie star had evidently felt it beneath him to do TV and to play a role other than a leading one. But the ratings of his last few movies had plummeted. Everyone who worked with him last season had been aware of his constant complaints. Eric was an egomaniac and a director's worst nightmare.

Rachel had managed to get along with Eric, but she couldn't say the same for others who considered him a pain in the rear end. But then, her older sister Sofia claimed Rachel could get along with just about anybody, and she would have to agree. It took a lot to rock her boat. She was easygoing by nature and was an all-around nice person. She figured some things just weren't worth the hassle of getting high blood pressure and stress.

A slight movement out of the corner of her eye made her shift her focus to the actor she'd heard would be added to the show this season in the role of Dr. Tyrell Perry. His name was Ethan Chambers.

He had been in Hollywood only a couple of years

and already, at twenty-eight, he had taken the town by storm. And most noticeably, over the past few months, he and his playboy behavior had become quite the talk in the tabloids and gossip columns.

She gave him an appreciative glance. The only thing she had to say was that if the producer added Ethan to the show to boost the ratings, then he had hit the mark. Ethan was definitely eye candy of the most delicious kind. There was no doubt in her mind he would stir the interest of their female viewers, young and old, single or married.

And she couldn't help noticing he had already stirred the interest of several of the females on the set. He seemed oblivious to the open stares as he talked to a man she assumed was his agent. Although she found Ethan extremely attractive, she was too much of a professional to mix her private life with her professional one. And the one thing she detested above all else was being in the spotlight, which was something he evidently enjoyed since he'd managed to garner a lot of publicity lately.

She thought that his flashing white smile was as sexy as they came and figured he would be perfect for any toothpaste commercial. He was tall, probably six foot two, and powerfully built with broad shoulders, muscled arms and a masculine chest. He did a whole lot for those scrubs he was wearing. The company that manufactured the medical attire should be grateful, since he practically turned them into a fashion statement.

And last but not least was his cocoa-colored face with those striking blue-gray eyes—a potentially distracting pair for any woman fool enough to gaze into them too long—and his ultrasexy dimpled jaw. She had to hand it to him, he was as handsome as any male could get in her book, hands down.

A soft smile lifted the corners of her lips as she thought that this was bound to be an interesting season. Already a number of the women on the set were vying for his attention. The show's director, Frasier Glenn, would just love that.

"Cut! Good scene, everyone. Let's move on!"

Frasier's words had Rachel moving quickly toward the producer, John Gleason, and Livia Blake, a model and budding actress who would be guest-starring on the show for a few episodes as Dr. Sonja Duncan. The scene they had just filmed was an emotional one in which Dr. Duncan had broken the news to a devoted husband that his wife had died of cardiac arrest.

Livia would be in the next scene as well and it was Rachel's job to refresh her hair and makeup. And since Rachel was also the wardrobe designer for the show, she needed to verify John's request for a change in the outfit Livia would be wearing in the scene they would be shooting later today.

Rachel flashed a look back to Ethan Chambers, and her gaze raked over him once again. The man by his side was doing all the talking, and for a quick moment she detected a jumpy tension surrounding Ethan. She had been around enough actors on their first day on the set to tell he was nervous. That surprised her. If anything, she would think a man with his looks would be brimming over with self-confidence, even arrogance. If he wasn't, than he was different from Eric Woods in more ways than one.

Ethan Chambers took another sip from the water bottle, wishing it was a cold beer instead. He couldn't believe he had finally gotten his lucky break and was here, on the set of *Paging the Doctor,* playing the role of a neurosurgeon. He wasn't a hospital maintenance man or a victim who needed medical care but a doctor. He had landed the role of a lifetime on what was one of the most top-rated shows.

He would even go so far as to pinch himself if there weren't so many people around, and if his agent, Curtis Fairgate, wasn't standing right next to him, smiling, gloating and taking it all in. And of course, Curtis was ready to take credit for the whole thing, as if Ethan hadn't worked his tail off to get where he was now.

He thought about the three years he had studied acting abroad while doing some well-received but small theater gigs. He could finally say he was now building an acting career. Even his older brother, Hunter, who had tried pressuring him to stay in the family business, was happy for him now. And that meant a lot.

"You do know your lines, don't you?"

Ethan lifted a brow, not believing Curtis would ask such a thing. "Of course. I might be nervous but I'm not stupid. I'm not about to screw up my big break."

"Good."

Ethan pulled in a slow breath, wondering how he and

Curtis had managed to survive each other for the past two years. Hollywood agents were known to be pushy, cynical and, in some cases, downright rude. Curtis was all three and then some. Ethan only kept him around because they had a fairly decent working relationship, and Curtis *had* managed to land him a spot on this show by talking to the right people. But Curtis probably would not have managed that if the sister of one of Ethan's former girlfriends hadn't been the current lover of one of the show's writers.

Curtis began talking, rambling on about something Ethan had no desire to listen to, so he glanced around, fascinated at how things were going and what people were doing. He had been on the set of a television show several times, but this was his first time on one that Frasier Glenn directed, and he couldn't help but admire how smoothly things were running. The word around Hollywood was that Frasier was a hard man to work for, a stickler for structure, but he was highly respected in the industry.

Ethan was about to pull his concentration back to the conversation he was supposed to be having with Curtis when his gaze settled on a gorgeous petite woman wearing a cute baby-doll top and a pair of wide-leg jeans. She was gorgeous in a restrained sort of way. He figured she was an actress on the show and wondered what role she played.

She couldn't be any taller than five foot two, but he thought she was a sexy little thing with her short dark hair and exotic looks. And she was smiling, which was a change of pace since everyone else seemed to look so doggone serious.

"Ethan!"

Curtis snapped his fingers in Ethan's face, cutting into his thoughts. "Don't even think it, Ethan," the man warned.

Ethan blinked, and an annoyed expression showed on his face as he met Curtis's gaze. "Think what?"

"About getting involved with anyone on this set, especially that hot little number over there. I know that look."

Ethan frowned. He liked women. He enjoyed sex. He did short-term affairs better than anyone he knew. The women he was involved with weren't looking for long-term any more than he was. "Why?" he finally asked.

"Frasier usually frowns on that sort of thing on his set, that's why."

Ethan took another sip of his water before asking, "Are you saying that he has a fraternization policy?"

"No, but a workplace romance isn't anything he gets thrilled about, trust me. It can cause unnecessary drama, and Frasier doesn't like drama since it can take away from a good day's work."

Ethan didn't say anything as his gaze found the object of his interest once again. For some reason, he had a feeling she would be worth any damn drama that got stirred. He shook his head, thinking he needed to put his player's mentality in check for a while, at least until the end of the season. Making his mark on this show was his goal, and now that he was in the driver's seat and pursuing his dream, the most important thing was for him to stay focused.

Although the urge to hit on the sexy pixie was strong, he would keep those longings in check. Besides, she probably wasn't even his type.

"I have a feeling you're going to be a big hit this season, Ethan."

Ethan glanced over at the woman who had introduced herself earlier as Paige Stiles, one of the production assistants. "Thanks."

"And like I said, if you ever need help with your lines after hours, just let me know. I will make myself available."

"I appreciate that, Paige." The offer seemed friendly enough, but he recognized it for what it was. The woman had been coming on to him ever since they had met earlier that day. She wasn't bad looking, in fact he thought her rather attractive; but she hadn't stirred his fire the same way the sexy pixie had.

Once the show had begun taping one scene after another, the petite brunette had all but disappeared. If she was an actress on the show then her segment was evidently being shot later. He was tempted to ask Paige who she was but thought better of it. The one thing a man didn't do was ask a woman who was interested in him about another woman.

"So where are we headed?" he asked as they moved away from the set toward an exit door.

"To the makeup trailer. That's also where wardrobe is located since the same person handles both."

He lifted a brow. "Is there a reason for that?" he asked, since that wasn't the norm, especially for a show of this magnitude. It was a lot of responsibility for one person.

"None other than that she wanted to do both, and Frasier obliged her. But he would since her last name happens to be Wellesley."

Ethan immediately recognized the last name. The Wellesleys were the brilliant minds behind Limelight Entertainment Management, one of the top talent agencies in the world. Their clientele consisted of some of the best in Hollywood, although in recent years they had expanded to represent more than actors. The firm now represented an assortment of talent that included big-name singers, set designers, costume designers, writers and makeup artists.

"Wellesley?" he asked.

"Yes, the high-and-mighty."

Ethan had the ability to read people, women in particular, and had easily detected the scorn in her voice. And because he knew about women in particular, he decided to change the subject. "How long have you worked for *Paging the Doctor?*"

She began talking and just as he'd done to Curtis earlier, he nodded while he tuned her out. His thoughts drifted back to the woman he'd seen earlier and he wondered if and when their paths would cross again and they would finally meet.

* * *

Finally a break, Rachel thought, sliding into a chair that was now empty. She had been in the trailer for the past five hours or so. She had sent one of her assistants out on the set to do those second-by-second touch-ups as needed while she hung out in the makeup/wardrobe trailer, making sure those actors shooting their scenes for the first time that day went through their initial makeup routine.

A couple of the scenes being shot today showed the doctors out of the hospital and in a more relaxed atmosphere either at home or out on dates, which called for a change from medical garments to casual wear.

John had approved her choice of outfits, and she felt good about that, especially since the outfit she'd selected for Livia hadn't been on John's preapproved list. And some of the artwork being used as props were her own creations. Other than Frasier and John, few people knew that when she left here at night she became Raquel, the anonymous canvas artist whose work was showcased in a number of galleries.

Her sister was worried that with being a makeup artist and wardrobe designer by day and a painter at night, Rachel had no time for a love life. But that was the least of Rachel's concerns. She was only twenty-six and wasn't ready for a serious involvement with any man.

In her early twenties she'd dated a lot, but to this day she couldn't admit to ever falling in love. She would like to believe such a thing could happen for her. Her aunt and uncle had a loving relationship, and she'd been told her parents had had one, too. Regrettably, they had been killed in a plane accident before her second birthday.

Rachel eased out of her chair when she heard conversation outside her door and glanced at the schedule posted on the wall. She wasn't supposed to work on anyone for another hour or so. Who could be infringing on her free time?

There was a knock on the trailer door, followed by a turn of the knob. Rachel fought to keep the frown off her face when Paige stuck her head in. The twenty-four-year-old woman had gotten hired during the middle of the first season. For some reason they had rubbed each other the wrong way that first day and things hadn't improved since. Rachel still didn't know the reason Paige disliked her, but figured it had to do with Rachel's amicable relationship with Frasier and John.

"So you're here," Paige said in a voice that for some reason gave Rachel the feeling Paige wished she wasn't.

Determined to present a friendly facade despite Paige's funky attitude, she smiled and said, "Yes, I'm here. Was there something you wanted?"

"Frasier wants to go ahead and shoot the next scene as soon as lunch is over, which means you need to get started on this guy right away."

Paige came inside the trailer, followed by the hunky and sexy Ethan Chambers. The moment Rachel's gaze clashed with those blue-gray eyes of his, she knew for the first time in her life how it felt to be totally mesmerized. And nothing could have prepared her for her hormones suddenly igniting into something akin to mind-blowing lust.

Chapter 2

So this was where his sexy pixie had gone to, Ethan thought, entering the trailer and glancing around. He pretended interest in everything inside the trailer except for the woman who'd been in the back of his mind since he'd first seen her that morning. And now here she was.

"Rachel, this is Ethan Chambers and starting this season he'll be a regular on the show as Dr. Tyrell Perry. Ethan, this is Rachel Wellesley, the makeup artist for the show. She's the wardrobe designer as well."

Again Ethan picked up a bit of scorn in Paige's voice, although she had a smile plastered on her face. But then it was evident her smile was only for him.

He crossed the room and extended his hand. "Nice meeting you, Rachel."

"Ditto, Ethan. Welcome to *Paging the Doctor.*"

The moment she placed her hand in his he was tempted to bring it to his lips, something he had gotten used to doing while living abroad in France. And when she smiled up at him the temptation increased. She had such a pretty smile.

"John wants him ready for his scene in thirty minutes. I'll be back to get him, so make sure he's on time."

Both Ethan and Rachel glanced over at Paige and watched as she exited the trailer, leaving them alone. Ethan returned his gaze to Rachel once again and couldn't help asking, "What's got her panties in a wad?"

Rachel couldn't help the laughter that flowed from her mouth, and when he joined in, she knew immediately she was going to like this guy. But then, what wasn't there to like?

Up close, Ethan Chambers was even more handsome than he had been across the room earlier. With him on the show, this would be a pretty good season. She couldn't wait to see them shoot his scene.

She finally answered him. "I have no idea," she said. "But we won't worry ourselves about it. My job is to get you ready for your scene."

"But what about your lunch? Shouldn't you be eating something?"

"I should be asking you the same thing, but to answer

your question, usually I bring lunch from home and eat while taking care of business matters," she said, thinking about the order she had downloaded off her iPhone. *Libby's,* an art gallery in Atlanta, had just requested several of her paintings to display.

He nodded. "I'm too nervous to eat so I asked if I could go ahead and get the makeup part taken care of. I apologize if I'm infringing on your time."

She waved off his words. "You're not, so just go ahead and take the chair while I pull your file."

"My file?"

"Yes. Sorry, I can be anal when it comes to being organized, but there's no other way to work with Frasier and John. I have a file of all the scenes you'll be doing today, what you'll need to wear and the extent of lighting needed for that particular shot, although the latter is definitely changeable on the set. That gives me an idea of what kind of makeup I need to apply."

She tried not to notice how he slid into the chair; specifically, how his muscular thighs straddled it before his perfectly shaped backside came in contact with the cushioned seat. She grabbed the folder off the rack and tried to ignore the dark hair that dusted his muscular arms. However, something caught her attention. A tattoo of a cluster of purple grapes draped above his wrist.

"Grapes?" she asked, meeting his gaze and finding it difficult to breathe while looking into his eyes.

"Yes. It's there to remind me of home."

"Home?" she echoed, breaking eye contact to reach over and hand him a smock to put on.

"Yes. Napa Valley."

She recalled the time she'd visited the area years ago as part of a high school field trip. "I've been to Napa Valley once. It's beautiful."

"Yes, it is. I hated leaving it," he said after putting on the smock.

She glanced over and met those killer eyes again. "Then why did you?"

He would be justified to tell her it wasn't her business, she quickly thought, but for some reason she knew he wouldn't do that. They had met just moments ago, but she felt she knew him, or knew men like him. No, she corrected herself. She didn't know any man like him, and how she could say that with such certainty, she wasn't sure.

"I left to pursue my dream. Unfortunately, it wasn't connected to my family business," he said.

Now that she understood. Her sister and uncle always thought she would join them in the family business, but she hadn't. Limelight Entertainment Management had been founded by her father, John Wellesley, and his brother Jacob. It had been the dream they shared and made into reality, with the purpose of representing and building the careers of African American actors during a time when there were many prejudices in Hollywood. Today the company was still very highly respected and had helped many well-known stars jumpstart their careers.

"It's a nice tattoo, but I'll need to use some cream to completely cover it for the shoot. Dr. Perry doesn't have a tattoo," she explained, pressing a button that eased the chair into a reclining position

"That's no problem. Do whatever you have to do, Rachel."

It wasn't what he'd said but how he'd said it that sent sensuous chills coursing through her. For a timeless moment, they stared at each other as heat flooded her in a way it never had before. As the flames of awareness licked at her body, somehow a part of her—the sensible part—remained unscathed. In a nagging voice it reminded her that she needed to get back on track and prep Ethan for his scene.

She swallowed and broke eye contact with him again as she turned to reach for her makeup kit. "Comfortable?"

"Yes."

"Then why are you so nervous?" she decided to ask him while checking different tubes of makeup cream for one that would work with his complexion and skin type. It was August, and although the air conditioner on the set would be on full blast, all the lighting being used would generate heat. She needed to prevent any facial shiny spots from showing up on camera.

He shifted in his seat and she glanced over at him. "This is the first day on the job of what I see as my big break," he said, straightening in the chair. "This is what I've worked my ass off for since the day I decided acting was what I wanted to do. I've done small parts in theater and guest spots on a couple of shows and was even an extra on *Avatar,* but being here, getting this opportunity, is a dream come true."

She nodded, knowing just how he felt. She had wanted to step out on her own without any help from her family's name. She had submitted her résumé to Glenn Productions and had gotten called in for an interview with both Frasier and John. Although Frasier had been a friend of her father's, and both men were well acquainted with Sofia since she was Uncle Jacob's partner in the family business, Rachel was convinced she had been given the job on her own merits and hadn't been given any preferential treatment.

This was her second season on the show and she worked doubly hard to make sure Frasier and John never regretted their decision to give her a chance. So, yes, she knew all about dreams coming true.

The first thing she thought as she applied a light brush to Ethan's face was that he had flawless skin with a healthy glow. He had perfect bone structure and his lips were shapely and full. She bent toward him to gently brush his brows and was glad he had closed his eyes since crazy things were going on in the pit of her stomach. A tightness was there that had never been there before. She drew in a deep breath to relieve the pressure. His aftershave smelled good. Almost too good for her peace of mind.

"So tell me, Rachel, what's your dream?"

She smiled. "What makes you think I have one?"

"All women do."

She chuckled. "Sounds like you think you know us pretty well."

"I wouldn't say that, but I would think everyone has at least one dream they would love to see come true."

"I agree, and this is mine—being a makeup artist and wardrobe designer."

"You're good at it. Very professional."

He opened his eyes to meet hers and she was aroused in a way that just wasn't acceptable, especially for a woman who made it her motto never to mix business with pleasure.

"Thanks," she said, taking a step back and reaching over to grab a hand mirror to give to him. "You didn't need much. I don't believe in being heavy-handed with makeup."

"I can appreciate that."

She had made up enough men in her day to know if they had a choice they would gladly skip this part in preparing for their scene. "Now for that tattoo. I have just the thing to blend in with your skin tone that won't rub off. And later you can wash it off."

"Okay."

He held out his arm and she began applying the cream. Against her fingertips, his skin felt warm, slowly sending her body into meltdown. She could feel his eyes on her but refused to glance up and look at him for fear that he would know what touching him was doing to her. Instead she tried concentrating on what she was doing. This time, though, she was too distracted by other things, such as the feel of his strong veins beneath her fingers and the rapid beat of his pulse. Her body responded with a raging flood of desire that seeped into her bones.

Not being able to resist temptation any longer, she looked over at him. For a long, achingly seductive moment, they stared at each other. She wanted to look away but it was as if he controlled the movement of her neck and it refused to budge. She swallowed the panic she felt lodged in her throat as she slowly released his hand. So much for being a firm believer in the separation of business and pleasure. For a moment, no matter how brief, thoughts had filled her mind about how it would be to take her hand and rub it down his chest and then move her hand even lower to—

There was a quick knock at the door before it opened and Paige walked in. And for the first time ever, Rachel was glad to see the woman.

Chapter 3

"If he's as hot as you say he is, then maybe you should let him know you might be interested, Rachel."

Rachel wiped paint from her hands as she glared at the phone. If her best friend since elementary school wasn't there in person to see her frown, transmitting it through the speakerphone was the next best thing. "I'm not interested."

And because she knew Charlene would belabor the point, she went on the defensive and said, "Look, Cha, I thought you of all people would understand. You know I don't like mixing business with pleasure. Besides, I have plenty of work to do."

Charlene laughed. "You always have plenty of work to do. If becoming involved with a man is a way to slow you down, then I'm all for it. It's time you started having fun."

Rachel rolled her eyes. "I could say the same for you."

"Face it. Men aren't drawn to me like they are to you."

Rachel pulled in a deep breath knowing there was no use telling Charlene just how wrong she was. Her words would go in one ear and out the other. For once she wished Charlene would be the one to face it and see that she was beautiful and sexy.

Charlene had to be the kindest and sweetest person Rachel knew, but she always slid to the background when it came to dating and romance. Rachel blamed Charlene's parents, since they always thought their older daughter, Candis, was the "pretty one" and had always put her in the limelight. As far as Rachel was concerned, Charlene had a lot going for her, including a beautiful singing voice.

"I'm in no mood to argue with you, Cha. You know how mad I get when you put yourself down."

"I'm not putting myself down. I'm just stating facts."

"Then let me state a few of my own," Rachel said. "I'm the one on set every day surrounded by gorgeous men. The only problem is that those men are checking out the tall, slender actresses, not me."

When Charlene didn't say anything, Rachel had a feeling there was more going on with her friend. "Okay, Cha, what's wrong?"

There was another long moment before Charlene replied, "I talked to Mom today."

Rachel slumped down into a chair. Mrs. Quinn was the mom from hell, and that was putting it kindly. She'd always managed to boost one daughter up while at the same time tearing the other one down. "And?"

"And she wanted me to know that Candis made the cut for the *Sports Illustrated* swimsuit edition next year and will be staying in Paris for a while."

"That's great, and I'm sure you're happy for her." Rachel knew she could say that because deep down she knew Charlene was. Candis and Charlene had a rather good relationship despite the competitive atmosphere created by their mother.

"Yes, of course I'm happy for her."

"And?"

"And what?" Charlene asked.

Rachel pulled in a deep breath; her patience was wearing thin. "And what else did Mrs. Quinn say?"

"Just the usual about she still doesn't understand how Candis could be so pretty and me so plain when we had the same parents. She ended the call by even suggesting that maybe she and Dad got the wrong baby from the hospital. She said it in a joking way but I knew she was dead serious."

Rachel bet the woman had been dead serious as well, but she would never tell Charlene that. That was the kind of garbage she'd had to put up with all her life. "She wasn't serious, Cha. You and your mother look too much alike for you to be anyone's baby but hers."

Evidently Mrs. Quinn never took the time to notice the similarity. Or maybe she *had* noticed and since she'd never been happy with her own looks, she was passing her insecurities on to Charlene.

Rachel thought about her own situation. She had been raised by her uncle Jacob and her aunt Lily after her parents had been killed. Rachel had been only one year old and Sofia had been ten. Her aunt and uncle were wonderful and had raised her and Sofia as their own children, since unfortunately they'd never had any. The one thing Uncle Jacob and Aunt Lily didn't do was play her and Sofia against each other. Everyone knew that Sofia wanted to follow in their father's footsteps and take his place with Uncle Jacob at Limelight.

Although her uncle and sister would have loved for her to join them in the family business, Rachel had never been pressured to do so. She chuckled, thinking it was enough to have Sofia as her agent.

"Hey, let's do a movie this weekend," she suggested, thinking her best friend needed some chilling time.

"Sounds super, but don't you have a lot to do?"

Rachel laughed. "I always have a lot to do, but I need a break to have fun, and it sounds like you do, too."

A short while later, Rachel made her way to the kitchen, hungry after missing lunch. On the way home she had stopped by a restaurant owned by one of the cameramen's parents. She considered Jack Botticello her buddy, and his parents were truly a godsend. Whenever she dropped by their Italian restaurant, Botticello's Place, for takeout, they always gave her more food than she could possibly eat in one sitting. There would definitely be enough lasagna left for tomorrow's dinner.

As she sat down at the table to enjoy her meal, she recalled everything that had happened on the set that day, especially the scenes that included Ethan Chambers. She couldn't help but remember the moment he had walked into a patient's hospital room. To say he swaggered into the room would probably be more accurate. And when he began speaking in what was supposed to be a northern accent, all eyes and ears were on him. There was no doubt in her mind he was a gifted actor. It was as if the part of Dr. Tyrell Perry had been created just for him.

She couldn't wait for the airing of the show in a few weeks to see how he would be received by the viewing audience. It would probably be no different than the way he'd been received on the set. Women were all but falling at his feet, doing just about anything to get his attention.

He had mentioned to a member of the camera crew in between scenes that he was going to get a cup of coffee. The three women who'd overheard him had all but broken their necks racing across the room to the coffee cart to get it for him. She could tell he'd actually gotten embarrassed by their antics. That surprised her. Most men would be gloating about all the attention. But then, this had been his first day on the job. There was no doubt in her mind that eventually his media-hungry playboy tendencies would come out. It was only a matter of time.

Unbidden, the memories surfaced of what had happened during their makeup session that day. Had he deliberately tried to unnerve her? Break down her defenses so she would behave the way Tina, Cindy and Nina had done today with the coffee incident? It wouldn't surprise her to discover he was just as superficial as all the other playboys in Hollywood. And to think for a short while today she'd actually been attracted to him. But with his make-you-drool looks, the attraction couldn't be helped. It had a way of vamping your senses the first time around.

And his family had money. He'd mentioned his roots were in Napa Valley, but it was only later that day when she'd overheard some of the camera crew talking about how wealthy he already was that she realized he was one of *those* Chamberses. There were two African American families whose roots and vast financial empires were in Napa Valley. The Russells and the Chamberses. Both families' vineyards were known to produce some of wine tasters' finest.

So, okay, she had let her guard down and let herself be affected by him. But tomorrow would be better. She had gotten used to him and would be more in control.

With that resolved, she proceeded to finish her meal.

"Do you promise, Uncle Ethan?"
Ethan couldn't help but smile. "Yes, I promise."
"Truly?"
"Yes, truly."

His six-year-old niece, Kendra, had him wrapped around her finger and probably knew it, he thought. When his parents had mentioned to her that Los Angeles was close to Disneyland, she had begun asking him questions. Mainly she wanted to know if he'd seen any princesses.

Just to hear her voice was a sheer delight because Kendra hadn't done much talking since her mother had died three years ago in a car accident. She had pretty much been withdrawn and quiet much of the time. But she would always talk to her Uncle Ethan.

"Daddy wants to talk to you, Uncle Ethan."

"Okay, sweetheart, and always remember you're Uncle Ethan's cupcake."

"I remember. Nighty-night."

He then heard her hand the phone over to his brother, Hunter, after telling her daddy nighty-night, too and after exchanging an "I love you" and an "I love you back." It was only then that Hunter placed the phone to his ear. "What's going on, kid?"

Ethan couldn't help but chuckle. There was an eight year difference in their ages, and Hunter never let him forget it. But even with that big variation, they'd always gotten along. Like all brothers, they'd had their disagreements, but they'd never lasted more than a few hours. Except for that one time a few years ago when Hunter had tried pressuring him into staying in the family business and getting all those ideas out of his head about making it big in Hollywood.

Ethan had left home anyway to pursue his dream.

It was only after the fatal car accident that claimed Hunter's wife's life—an accident that Hunter and Kendra had survived—that Hunter had understood why Ethan had to do what he did. He'd learned that life was too precious and fleeting to take for granted. Tomorrow wasn't promised to anyone.

"Nothing much is going on. Kendra talked a lot tonight," he said.

"Only because it's you. She loves her uncle Ethan. Besides, she wanted to ask you all about princesses."

Ethan grinned. "Yeah, I noticed. What's up with that?"

"*The Princess and the Frog.* She's seen it five times already. I should blame you since you're the one who got her the DVD as soon as it went on sale."

"Hey, there's nothing I wouldn't do for my cupcake," he said, meaning it.

He talked to Hunter for a few minutes longer before his brother passed the phone to their folks. In addition to the winery, Hunter and his parents ran a small four-star bed-and-breakfast on the property. It was always good to call home because he truly missed everyone, and updates were priceless.

"And you're eating properly, Ethan?"

He cringed at his mother's question, knowing he would have to tell her a little white lie, especially when at that very moment the timer went off to let him know his microwave dinner was ready. He had a beer to drink and his dessert would be a bag of peanut M&M's he'd grabbed out of the vending machine when he'd left the studio today. Paige had invited him to her place for dinner but he had declined.

He removed his dinner from the microwave and said, "Yes, Mom, I'm eating properly."

"Met any nice girls you want to bring home?"

She has to be kidding. The last few girls he dated weren't any he would dare bring home for his parents, brother and niece to meet. But then the face of his sexy pixie flashed across his mind and he couldn't help but think that she would work. For some reason he liked her, and the sexual vibes between them hadn't gone unnoticed, although it was evident she'd tried ignoring them.

Besides, he didn't have time to meet girls—nice or any other kind. He had lines to study every night, especially tonight. Frasier had been impressed with him today and had added another scene to his schedule for tomorrow.

"No, Mom, so don't go planning a wedding for me yet."

Later that night when he slid into bed, he couldn't help but think just how blessed he was. Both of his parents were alive and in good health. As the oldest son, Hunter had taken on his role with ease and was the perfect businessman to manage the family's vast wealth. And Hunter had had the insight to utilize the property surrounding the winery to build the bed-and-breakfast, which was doing extremely well. The reservation list was always filled up a year in advance.

As much as he'd loved Napa Valley, Ethan had

known it wasn't in his blood to the extent it had been in Hunter's. After college, he returned home and tried working alongside Hunter and his parents, but he hadn't been happy. Hunter had said it was wanderlust and that eventually he would get over it, but he never did. A year later he had made up his mind to pursue his dream.

So here he was, living in a nice place in L.A. and building the career he'd always wanted. Money was no object, thanks to a trust fund that had been set up by his grandparents as well as the financial standing of the winery, in which he was a stockholder. Of course, every once in a while some smart-ass reporter would ask him why an independently wealthy person would want to work. He was sure Anderson Cooper was asked the same question often enough, too. Ethan wasn't privy to Anderson's response, but his was simply, "Wealthy or poor, everyone has dreams, and there *is* such a thing as continued money growth."

He reached over to turn off the lamp light, thinking that things had gone better than he'd expected on the set today. His lines had flowed easily, and for a while he had stepped into the role of Dr. Tyrell Perry. To prepare, he had watched medical movies and had volunteered his time at a hospital for ninety days. He had come away with an even greater respect for those in the medical industry.

As he stared up at the ceiling his thoughts shifted to the woman he'd met that day, Rachel Wellesley. There had been something about her that pulled her to him like a magnet. Something about her that he found totally adorable. Even among the sea of model-type women on the set, she had somehow stood out.

And when she had leaned over him to apply whatever it was she brushed on his face, he had inhaled her scent. With his eyes closed, he had breathed it all in while imagining all sorts of things. It was a soft scent, yet it had been hot enough to enflame his senses.

So he had sat there, letting her have her way with his face while he imagined all kind of things, especially the image of her naked.

More than once during the shoot, he had had to remind himself that he didn't really know her and that it would be crazy to lose focus. But he would be the first to admit that he hadn't counted on being bowled over by a woman who had to tilt her head all the way back just to look up at him. He smiled, remembering the many times they had looked at each other and the number of times they had tried not to do so. And nothing could erase from his mind the sight of the soft smile that had touched her lips when she'd seen his tattoo and when he'd told her why he had it. If he had been trying to impress her, he would definitely have garnered brownie points. But he wasn't trying to impress her.

He shifted in bed, knowing he had to stay focused and not let a pretty face get him off track. All that sounded easy enough, but he had a feeling it would be the hardest thing he'd ever had to do.

Chapter 4

"Quiet on the set!

"Take four!

"Action!"

Rachel sat quietly in a chair and watched the scene that was being shot. When she heard two women, Paige and another actress on the set named Tae'Shawna Miller, whispering about how handsome and fine Ethan was, she had to press her lips together to keep from turning around and reminding them about the no-talking-during-a-take policy. But that would make her guilty of breaking the rule, too.

So she sat there and tried tuning them out and hoped sooner or later they would close their mouths. It didn't help matters to know that Paige was one of the women. Rachel figured she of all people should know better.

Rachel turned her attention back to the scene being filmed and couldn't help but admire the way Ethan was delivering his lines. He was doing a brilliant job portraying Dr. Tyrell Perry, the sexy doctor with a gruff demeanor that could only be softened by his patients. And from the looks of things, a new twist was about to unravel on the show with Dr. Perry being given a love interest—another new doctor on the hospital staff, the widowed Dr. Sonja Duncan.

Rachel had been on the set talking to one of the cameramen when Ethan arrived that morning, swaggering in and exuding rugged masculinity all over the place. The number of flirtatious smiles that were cast his way the moment he said good morning had only made her shake her head. Some of the women were probably still wiping the drool from their mouths.

Why did women get so silly at the sight of a good-looking man? She would admit she had been attracted to him yesterday like everyone else, after all she was a woman, but there was no reason to get downright foolish about it.

"Freeze! No talking on the set!"

Frasier was looking straight at Paige and Tae'Shawna and frowning. He knew exactly who the noisemakers were, and to be called out by the director wasn't good. They had caused time to be wasted, and everyone knew Frasier didn't like that.

"Unfreeze!"

This time around, everyone was quiet while the shooting of the scene continued. In this scene, Dr. Tyrell Perry and Dr. Sonja Duncan were discussing the seriousness of a patient's condition. It was obvious in this scene that the two were attracted to each other. The television viewers would already know through the use of flashbacks that Sonja's late husband, also a doctor, had gotten killed when an L.A. gang, intent on killing a man being treated in the hospital, burst into the E.R. and opened fire, killing everyone, including the doctor, a nurse and a few others waiting to be treated.

Rachel figured since Livia was only a temporary member of the cast, there would not be too much of a budding romance between the two doctors, although it wasn't known just how Livia's exit would be handled. Frasier was known to leave the viewers hanging from scene to scene, so it would be anyone's guess what he had in mind. She couldn't help but wonder if the chemistry the two generated on the set would extend beyond filming.

She hadn't gotten a chance to get to know Livia. During the makeup and wardrobe sessions there hadn't been much conversation between them. Her initial impression was that Livia was just as shallow and self-absorbed as the other Hollywood types Rachel had met. She'd seen no reason for that impression to change. Livia had a reputation of being a party girl and as much the tabloid princess as Ethan was the tabloid king. So it would stand to reason the two would be attracted to each other both on and off the set.

"Cut! Good scene! Let's enjoy lunch. Everyone take an additional hour and be back to start again on time."

Rachel smiled, grateful for the extra time. It seemed a number of people were in a hurry to take advantage of Frasier's generosity…in more ways than one, she thought, when out of the corner of her eye she noticed several women bustling over in Ethan's direction. She rolled her eyes. My goodness, did they have no shame? Interestingly, Livia walked away in another direction, as if the attention given to Ethan didn't concern her one bit.

Shaking her head, Rachel walked back to her trailer to grab her purse. She had a few errands to do before lunch was over.

Ethan watched Rachel leave before forcing his attention back to the two women standing in front of him. Tae'Shawna had all but invited him over tonight to go skinny-dipping in her pool. Of course he had turned her down. Paige had offered to come over to his place to help him go over his lines. He turned her down as well. For some reason, he wasn't feeling these two. If truth be told, he wasn't feeling any woman right now. Except for the one who'd just headed off toward her trailer.

"So what are you doing for lunch, Ethan? We would love for you to join us," Paige invited, interrupting his thoughts.

"Thanks, but I have a few errands I need to take care of," he said, knowing it was a lie as he said it. But in this case, he felt it was justified.

"No problem. Maybe we can help with your errands and—"

"Thanks again, but that's not necessary," he said, pulling his keys out of his back pocket. He had planned to wait until the weekend to shop for Kendra's gift, but now was just as good a time since these two were beginning to make a nuisance of themselves.

"I'll see you ladies later. I need to leave so I can be back on time."

For a second Paige looked like she was going to invite herself along. Instead she said, "Then I guess we'll see you when you return."

He only smiled, refusing to make any promises as he headed toward the exit. He was grateful for the additional hour and planned on making good use of it. Moving quickly, he reached for the door at the same time someone else did. The moment their hands touched he knew the identity of that person. Her scent gave her away.

"Excuse me."

"Excuse me as well," he said, taking a step back, opening the door and holding it for her to pass through. "You're taking advantage of the extra hour, I see."

Rachel smiled up at him. "I think everyone is." She glanced back over his shoulder. "Where's your fan club?"

His gaze scanned over her face and he saw a cute little mole near the corner of her lip. How could he have missed it yesterday? "My fan club?"

"Yes."

They were walking together as they headed toward the parking lot. "Trust me, there are some fans you can do without."

"And you want me to believe you're not flattered?" she teased, speaking in a low tone when a crew member passed them on the sidewalk.

He slowed his pace as they got closer to where the cars were parked in the studio lot. "Yes, that's exactly what I want you to believe."

She stopped walking and so did he. "Why? Why does it matter what I think?"

Ethan thought she had asked a good question. Why did it matter what she thought? He knew the answer before he could pull in his next breath. He liked her, and if he had the time he would try to get something going with her. The thing was he didn't have the time. He had to stay focused and doubted he would have time to pursue a relationship, serious or otherwise, with any woman anytime soon. He kept reminding himself that this was his big break, and he wasn't about to mess it up by trying to get between any woman's legs. He had gone without for six months, and he could go another six months or more if he had to.

But that didn't mean that he and Rachel couldn't be just friends, did it? It would be nice to have someone who wasn't interested in anything more than friendship. The little attraction that had passed between them yesterday couldn't be helped. After all, she was a nice-looking woman and he was a hot-blooded man. But as long as they kept things under control, being just friends would be fine.

"It matters because I like you and I'd like for us to be friends," he said.

She pushed a wayward strand of hair from her face as she looked at him. "And why would you want us to become friends?"

Providing an answer to that question was easy enough. "The one thing I noticed yesterday was that you're genuinely a nice person." He chuckled then added, "Hey, you didn't rag on me about being nervous. And it's obvious everyone on the set likes you, from the maintenance man all the way up to the bigwigs. I figure with that kind of popularity, you can't be all bad. Besides, you and Livia are the only two females on the set that I feel pretty comfortable around."

She lifted a brow. "Livia?"

"Yes."

She tilted her head back as if to give him her full attention. "Not that it is any of my business, but I thought that maybe something was going on between the two of you."

He smiled. "There is, on the show. But it's all acting. She's supposed to be my new love interest for the next few episodes."

She nodded. "Your scenes earlier were pretty convincing."

He chuckled. "We're actors. They were meant to be convincing."

Ethan glanced at his watch. "I'd better get going. I

want to pick up something for my six-year-old niece from the Disney Store. After watching *The Princess and the Frog* she's into princesses, so I thought I'd pick her up a Princess Tiana doll."

A smile touched the corners of her lips. "You have a niece?"

"Yes, Kendra. She's my older brother's little girl and, I hate to say it, but she's perfect."

She chuckled. "I believe you. And there's a store in walking distance on Hollywood Boulevard. I'm headed that way myself to pick up something from the art supply shop."

He turned the idea over in his mind only once before asking, "Mind if I tag along?"

He did his best not to watch the way her lips were tugged up in a smile when she said, "Sure, you can tag along, as long as we don't talk about work. We need to give our brains a break."

He jammed his keys in his pocket as he resumed walking by her side. It was a beautiful August day, and he had a beautiful woman strolling alongside him. Things couldn't get any better than that. "So what do we talk about?" he decided to ask her.

She slanted her head to look at him. "You."

"Me?"

"Yes."

"Hey, we talked about me yesterday."

Her mouth twitched in a grin. "Yes, but all I know is that you're from Napa Valley and you have a niece."

She chuckled. "I guess I could go by what I've heard and—"

"Read in the tabloids," he said, finishing the statement for her.

"No, I don't do tabloids. It would be nice if others didn't do them either, then they would go out of business."

He glanced over at her and laughed. "You don't like the right of free speech?"

She laughed back at him. "More like the right of sleazy speech. Ninety percent of what they print isn't true, but then I guess that's the price of being a star."

He smiled, liking the way the sunlight was bouncing off her hair, making it appear even more lustrous. He liked the short cut on her. "Yes, it's one of the detriments, that's for sure. I just go with the flow. As long as I know what's true about me and what's not, I don't lose any sleep."

She didn't say anything for a while, and then replied, "I hate being in the spotlight."

She kept looking ahead, but he'd heard what she said. Clearly. If that was true, he wondered how she managed it, being a Wellesley. The company her family owned was so connected with this industry, and had been for close to thirty years, they were practically an icon in Hollywood.

He had researched information on Limelight when he'd returned to the States from abroad. He had even considered contacting them to handle his affairs before he'd chosen Curtis, who'd been a friend of a friend to whom he'd owed a favor. But he wouldn't hesitate to consider them again when his contract with Curtis ended. Lately, he'd begun feeling as if he was making his own contacts. Everyone he knew handled by Limelight was pleased with its services. Not once had they ever been made to feel like they were a passenger instead of a driver.

"Being in the spotlight doesn't bother me," he decided to say. "It comes with the territory. But then, my family is well-known in Napa Valley, so I got used to having a mike shoved in my face, only to be quoted incorrectly." He could recall a number of times when he'd been referred to as "the playboy Chambers" while Hunter had always been considered the one with a level head. The responsibly acting Chambers.

"And it doesn't bother you?" she asked.

He met her gaze. "A distortion of the truth will bother most people, and I'm no different. However, I don't lose sleep over it," he said, shifting his gaze to study her features.

But he had a feeling she would.

There had to be a reason, and the question rested on the tip of his tongue.

But he had no right to pry. This woman owed him nothing, had no reason to divulge her deep, dark secrets and innermost feelings. Not to him. They weren't husband and wife. They weren't even lovers. Nor would they ever be.

No, he reminded himself, he was trying out the friendship thing.

Chapter 5

Rachel could feel the power of Ethan as he walked beside her. And although it sounded strange, she could feel his strength. Not only did she feel it, she was drawing from it.

The very thought that such a thing was possible should be disconcerting, but instead the knowledge seemed to wrap her in some sort of warm embrace. That in itself was kind of weird since they'd decided to just be friends. She was fine with that decision. In fact, she refused to have things any other way. She didn't mix business with pleasure and she had too much on her plate to become involved in a serious relationship.

The last guy she had gone out with that she'd truly liked had been Theo Lovett. That had been a couple of years ago. They had dated for almost six months before she'd found out the only reason he'd been interested in her was as a way into her family's business. Luckily, she'd overheard him bragging to a friend on the phone when he'd thought she was in the shower and out of hearing range. Theo's explanation that he'd only been joking with his friend hadn't made her change her mind when she had kicked him out that day.

She stepped out of her memory and into the present. Apparently she'd missed some of what Ethan had said while she'd been daydreaming, because he'd changed the subject and was talking about his family.

"My older brother's name is Hunter. There is an eight year difference in our ages."

She glanced over at him. Despite the fact he was a lot taller than she, walking side by side they seemed to fit, and their steps appeared to be perfectly synchronized. How was that possible with his long legs and her short ones? He'd evidently adjusted his steps to stay in sync with hers. It was a perfectly measured pace.

"There is a nine year difference in me and my sister's ages," she said.

"Really? Was your sibling as overprotective as mine while you were growing up?"

Rachel made a face. "Boy, was she ever. She was ten when our parents were killed in a plane crash, and I was one. Our aunt and uncle became our legal guardians, but somewhere along the way my sister, Sofia, thought I became her responsibility. It was only when she left for college that I got some breathing space."

"Are the two of you close now?"

"Yes, very. What about you and your brother? Are the two of you close?"

"Yes, although I would be the first to admit he was somewhat of a pain in the ass while we were growing up. But I can appreciate it now since he covered for me a lot with my parents."

She could imagine someone having to do that for him. She had a feeling he'd probably been a handful. "Was your family upset when you decided not to enter the family business but to forge a path in a different direction?"

The corners of his lips lifted in a wry smile. "Let's just say they weren't thrilled with the idea. But I think it bothered Hunter more than it did them," he said. "The Chamberses have been in the wine business for generations, and I was the first to pull out and try doing something else. He lay on the pressure for me to stay for a while but then he backed off."

He placed his hand at the center of her back when others, walking at a swifter pace than they, moved to pass them. She could feel the warmth of his touch through her blouse. She breathed in deeply at the feeling of butterflies flapping around in her stomach.

"What about your family?" he inquired, not realizing the effect of his touch on her.

"Once I explained things to Uncle Jacob and Aunt Lily, they were fine with it. They wanted me to do whatever made me happy. But Sofia felt it was part of our father's legacy, that I owed it to him to join her and

Uncle Jacob at Limelight. I had made up my mind on how I wanted to do things with my future, so instead of letting there be this bone of contention between us, she backed off and eventually gave me her blessings to do whatever I wanted to do with my life."

She chuckled. "As a concession, I am letting Limelight Entertainment handle my career. I'm one of their clients."

They paused a moment when they reached the security gate. They had deliberately walked the expanse of the studio lot to avoid running into the paparazzi that made the place their regular beat. Now that they were no longer in safe and protected territory, she noticed Ethan had slid on a pair of sunglasses. He had kept on his medical scrubs and had a stethoscope around his neck, and she wondered if anyone seeing him would assume he was a bona fide doctor walking the strip on lunch break.

She pulled her sunglasses out of her bag, too, although it had been years since she'd had the paparazzi on her tail. When she was younger, they'd seemed to enjoy keeping up with the two Wellesley heirs. She'd always found the media's actions intrusive and an invasion of her privacy. She could recall all the photographs of her as a child that had appeared in the tabloids. That was the main reason she much preferred not being the focus of their attention again.

She glanced over at Ethan when his hand went to the center of her back again. It was time for them to cross the street, and he was evidently trying to hurry her along before traffic started up again. Her pulse began fluttering, caused by the heat generated from his touch.

They increased their pace to make it across the street. She checked him out from the corner of her eye and saw how sexy the scrubs looked on him. They had agreed to be just friends, she reminded herself. And it meant absolutely nothing that they had a few things in common. Like the fact that they were both renegades. That they were both members of well-known families. That they both had siblings who'd chosen to go into the family business. Overprotective, older siblings who meant well but if given the chance would run their lives.

Rachel inconspicuously scanned the area around them and breathed a sigh of relief when she saw the paparazzi was nowhere in sight. But then they were known to bounce out from just about any place. Hopefully she and Ethan looked like a regular couple out on a stroll during their lunch hour.

A couple who were just friends, which was something she could not forget.

"You are such a good uncle."

Ethan glanced at Rachel while accepting his change from the girl behind the counter at the Disney Store. Had he used his charge card his cover would have been blown. Even through his sunglasses, he could see the woman was looking at him, trying to figure out if he was a doctor or someone she should know.

He smiled at Rachel. "I'd like to think so, especially

since I doubt very seriously that Hunter will have any more children," he said, accepting the bag the cashier was handing him.

"Why is that?"

"He lost his wife in a car accident," he explained as they headed for the exit. "He took Annette's death hard and hasn't been in a serious relationship since. It's been three years now."

"Oh, how sad."

"Yes, it was. Hunter and Kendra were in the car at the time of the accident and survived with minor injuries," he said. He paused a moment and then added, "Kendra was three at the time and very close to her mother. She felt the loss immediately and withdrew into her own world and stopped talking."

The eyes that stared into his were full of sorrow and compassion. "She doesn't talk?"

He released his breath in a long and slow sigh, wondering why he was sharing this information about his family with anyone, especially to a woman he'd only met yesterday. But there was something about Rachel that was different from most women he'd met. For one, she wasn't trying to come on to him or jump his bones. It was as if she saw him as a person and not some sex symbol, and he appreciated that.

"She talks now, but not as much as she should for a child her age," he responded. "And she talks more with some people than with others. I happen to be one of those she will talk to most of the time. But it took me a while to gain that much ground again after the accident." He recalled the time he had come home from France to give his brother and niece his support. "But a part of Kendra is still withdrawn and so far no one has been able to fully bring her back. She's been seen by the best psychologists money can hire. They practically all said the same thing. Kendra suffered a traumatic loss, and until she's convinced in her mind that she can love someone again, become attached to that person without losing them all over again, she will continue to withdraw into her own little world."

He checked his watch and figured they needed to head on back. Prior to stopping at the store, they had stopped by an art supply place and picked up some new brushes. She'd told him that she liked dabbling with paints on canvas every once in a while and had promised to show him some of her work one day.

As they began retracing their steps back toward the studio lot, he had to admit he had enjoyed his time with her and knew that he was going to enjoy having her as a friend. An odd thought suddenly burned in his brain. What if they became more than just friends? He quickly forced the notion out of his head. The fact of the matter was they were just friends, or at least they were trying to be.

He glanced at her and saw her scan the surrounding area. He could tell she was nervous about the possibility of being seen by the paparazzi. So was he, but only because it bothered her. Despite the fact that only minutes ago he'd vowed not to pry, he couldn't stop the question now.

"Why do you avoid the spotlight, Rachel?" He could tell his question surprised her and suspected her reasons were deep-seated.

"I just do," she said.

She tried to act calm, like his question wasn't a big deal, but he sensed that it was. "Why?"

She frowned up at him, and the first thing he thought was that he'd made her mad. He hadn't meant to, but a part of him wanted to push her for an answer.

"Well?" he asked.

She didn't say anything as they kept walking. She had stopped glaring at him and was staring straight ahead. He'd almost given up hope for a reply when she began speaking. "I told you my parents were killed before my second birthday. Since my uncle and aunt who adopted us couldn't have any kids of their own, my sister and I became known as the Limelight heirs. For some reason we made news, and the paparazzi followed us practically everywhere we went—school, church, grocery stores… you name it, they were there. I couldn't tell you how many times when I was a little girl that I got a mike shoved in my face or my braid pulled by a reporter to get my attention. It was…scary.

"Things only got better when I went away to college. By the time I returned, the media interest was on someone else, thank goodness. But every once in a while someone tries to connect the dots to see what Sofia and I are up to. She doesn't mind being in the spotlight and uses it to her advantage."

Ethan took in what she said. The thought of someone

harassing a child to get a story angered him, and knowing the child had been Rachel angered him even more. It was interesting that he felt such protective instincts for her.

A flicker of some sort of alarm flashed through his brain but he chose to ignore it. No matter what his mind thought, there was no way he would get in too deep with Rachel.

Chapter 6

Rachel stood by the window in her uncle's study and gazed out at the ocean. The sun was going down and she enjoyed watching it. Just like she had enjoyed being on the set the past two weeks.

Frasier and John were pleased with the tempo of the series. Ethan was working out perfectly as Dr. Perry, and the blossoming on-the-air love affair between the gruff doctor and the resistant Dr. Duncan had pretty much heated up. They had shot a love scene yesterday that had pushed the temperature on the set up as hot as it could get for prime-time programming.

She could definitely say she was pleased with this assignment and looked forward to going into work each day. The more time she and Ethan spent together during filming, the more they talked and bonded as friends. She found him fun to be around, and the two of them would laugh together about some of the actresses' hot pursuit of him. A few had tried some outlandish things to get his attention. Like the time Jasmine Crowder summoned him to her trailer to help rehang a photo that had fallen off the wall. Instead of going, Ethan had sent one of the cameramen, Omar Minton, in his place. Poor Omar had walked into the trailer to be met by a half-naked Jasmine draped across the sofa.

That had been just one of many times during the past week that Ethan had had to foil seduction plots. Just the fact that he'd done so impressed Rachel, and she would be the first to admit that she was seeing him not as the superficial playboy she'd originally thought he was but as a focused, hardworking actor. That was another thing they had in common. They believed in professionalism on the job.

"Lily said I'd probably find you in here."

Rachel turned at the sound of her uncle's deep voice and smiled. Since she'd been only one year old when her parents had gotten killed, she didn't have a solid memory of them the way Sofia did. But what she did remember was her aunt and uncle being there for them, raising her and Sofia as their own. Rachel appreciated having been part of a family in which she'd always known she was loved and always been encouraged to use her talents in whatever way she wanted to do.

She'd learned from her aunt and uncle that her mother was a successful artist, and several of Vivian Wellesley's paintings were on the walls in this house as well as in a number of art galleries across the country. Vivian had passed down her talent and love of painting; Rachel really enjoyed the time she spent putting color to canvas. She was definitely her mother's daughter.

And Sofia was definitely her father's. She had stepped into the role of the savvy and successful businessman that he'd been. And because Sofia had been the only child for almost nine years, she had been the pride of her parents' life and definitely the apple of her father's eye. Sofia had worshipped the ground their father had walked on and was still doing that same thing even though their parents had been dead for twenty-five years. Sofia thought John Wellesley was the most amazing person to have ever lived.

The man standing before Rachel was John's identical twin.

"Uncle Jacob," Rachel greeted, crossing the room to give her uncle a hug. She'd seen pictures of the brothers from years past, and to see one was to see the other. That said, she knew if her father had lived he would have matured into a rather handsome man. And at fifty-five, her uncle was definitely that, with a charm and charisma that should be patented. Ethan had told her about the close relationship he had with his niece, and she had fully understood because such a relationship existed between her and her uncle.

"And what honor has been bestowed upon me for this visit?" he asked, leaning back and scanning her from head to toe. "Hmm, I don't see anything broken or in need of repair, although I still keep plenty of bandages around."

Rachel could only laugh. While growing up she had been a handful, a tomboy in her earlier years. And anytime she got hurt, she would run to her uncle to fix her boo-boo.

"C'mon, Uncle Jacob, it's not like I never come to visit," she defended herself, laughing.

"No, but since you've moved to the other side of town we barely see you these days."

Rachel nibbled on her bottom lip. In addition to the enormous mansion her aunt and uncle owned in Beverly Hills, they also had this place, a luxurious oceanfront hideaway on Malibu Beach. A few months ago she had purchased a condo in the gated community of Friar Gate that was located on the outskirts of Hollywood. Before moving, she had lived in a condo that had been within walking distance of Rodeo Drive. It was fine until one of the Jonas Brothers had moved into the complex. There was no peace with the paparazzi, and she'd figured it was just a matter of time before they added others to their list to harass.

"I needed more space," she said and knew her uncle would understand. It was no secret she didn't like being in the spotlight.

He nodded. "And when will I get invited to your new place for dinner?"

She threw her head back and laughed again, knowing that was a joke since she didn't cook. The few times she'd tried, she had made a complete mess of things and decided there were too many restaurants serving good, tasty food to put herself through the agony of following some recipe.

"Just as soon as I get everything in its proper place. I still have a few boxes left to unpack, but I've been so busy on the set. And then there's that painting I want to finish before the gallery hosts that charity event next month."

"I understand," Jacob Wellesley said, leading her to the nearest sofa so they could sit down. "You are a very busy lady, just like your mother was. We would try and convince her there were but so many hours in the day, but she was always determined to stretch them anyway."

Rachel couldn't help but smile. She always liked hearing the stories her uncle and aunt would share about her parents.

"And how are things going for you at work? Frasier isn't working you too hard, is he?" he asked.

Frasier Glenn was not only an old friend of her father's but he'd been close to her uncle as well and had been one of Limelight's first clients. When she'd interviewed for the position of makeup artist and wardrobe designer for *Paging the Doctor,* Frasier had been up-front and let her know it was her own merit and work ethic, not the long-standing friendship he had with her family, that had gotten her the job. She had appreciated that.

"No, both Frasier and John are wonderful, and I'm learning so much from them," she said, leaning back against the sofa's cushions.

"Good. I understand Eric Woods's contract didn't get renewed."

"No, but we were expecting it with his behavior last season. I hear he's mouthing off to the tabloids that he had no idea he was getting the ax."

Jacob shook his head. "Oh, I'm sure he knew. Frasier doesn't work that way. When he makes a decision to let you go, you know why. Eric's just trying to save face. Everyone in the industry knows his last few movies bombed out, and because of his temperament, it's hard to find a director in Hollywood with the patience to take him on."

Rachel nodded. "This season is going to have a new twist. They brought in a new doctor and I think his appearance will boost ratings."

"Really? Who is he?"

"Ethan Chambers."

A slow smile touched Uncle Jacob's lips. "I've never met Chambers but I've heard of him. Word's out that he's an actor who's going places. He received good reviews from the guest spot he did on CSI that one time last year. And there was that rumor earlier this year that he was being considered for *People*'s Sexiest Man of the Year. That didn't hurt. There hasn't been an African American male to get that honor since Denzel and that was close to fifteen years ago."

Rachel could see Ethan being considered. He was definitely a hot contender in her book.

"And how is Chambers working out?"

"I think he's doing a great job. It is difficult, though,

to get the females on the set to concentrate on what they are supposed to do instead of on him. He has a way of grabbing your attention and holding it."

"Mmm, does he now?"

She smiled, knowing what her uncle was probably thinking. "Okay, I admit he's hot, but I'm beyond fawning over any man, Uncle Jacob. Besides, Ethan Chambers comes with something I could never tolerate."

Jacob Wellesley lifted a thick brow. "What?"

"The spotlight."

Later that night, after spending time in front of the canvas for a good part of the evening, Rachel's phone rang. She reached out and picked it up without checking caller ID, thinking it was either Charlene or Sofia.

"Hello?"

"Save me."

She blinked upon hearing the sound of the ultrasexy, masculine voice. "Ethan?"

"Yes, it's me."

She was surprised. They had known each other for two weeks now, considered themselves friends and had even exchanged phone numbers one day on the set, but he'd never called her before and she'd never had a reason to call him. And what was his reason for calling her now? Had he said something about saving him?

"What on earth is going on with you?" she asked, putting him on speakerphone while she dried her hands.

"I need a place to crash for the night. I came home

and found the place swarming with paparazzi. Luckily they didn't see me, and I made a U-turn and headed in another direction. So, will you have pity on me and put me up for the night?"

She tossed the hand towel aside as she leaned against the kitchen counter. "Ethan, you know how I detest being—"

"In the spotlight. Yes, I know," he said interrupting her. "And that's the reason I hesitated calling you, but I need this favor, Rachel. I've been driving around for a few hours now and have periodically checked my rearview mirror to make sure no one is following me. They're probably still parked out front waiting for me to come home. They wouldn't think of looking for me at your place."

That was an understatement, Rachel thought. They probably figured he was somewhere warming some starlet's bed. He was single, sexy and a man who probably had needs that any woman would love filling. In that case, why couldn't he go back to his lady friend's place instead of putting her privacy at risk?

She began nibbling on her bottom lip. Tomorrow was Sunday and they were due back on the set Monday morning at eight. All she needed was for someone to get wind that Ethan had stayed overnight at her place, no matter how innocent it might be, and make a big deal of it.

Everyone on the set knew the two of them had become friends, but no one thought anything of it since she was friendly with just about everyone…except for Paige, who still had her panties in a wad for some reason. Besides, no one would assume something was going on between them because she wasn't the type of woman Ethan would be interested in. She was definitely not model material.

But still, she didn't want anyone assuming anything or, even worse, the paparazzi hunting him down at her place. Jeez, she didn't want to even think of that happening. One good thing was that she had a two-car garage, so his car wouldn't be seen parked in front of her place. And her gated community was known for its privacy and security.

"Rachel?"

She drew in a deep breath. "Fine, but if anyone from the media gets wind of this and starts harassing me, Ethan, you're dead meat."

She heard him laugh. "I don't want to be dead meat, Rachel."

She folded her arms across her chest and tapped her foot. "Well?"

"All right, I'll take my chances."

"With the paparazzi?"

"Heck no," he said. "I'll take my chances with you. I'm hoping our budding friendship will keep you from actually killing me. Besides, I've been around you enough to know that you do have a soft heart."

She either had a soft heart or a foolish mind, Rachel thought an hour later when she opened her door to Ethan. She also had a bunch of erratic hormones. The tingle started in the pit of her stomach when she looked at him, and it took a full minute to catch her breath. Not only did Ethan look good but he smelled good enough to eat.

She was caught off guard by her reaction to him. They'd agreed to just be friends, but at the moment friendship was the last thing on her mind. She couldn't stop her gaze from roaming all over him. He was leaning in the doorway in a sexy stance, wearing jeans and a button-down shirt with the top four buttons undone. She glimpsed his chest beneath, poking out like a temptation being dangled in front of her. If this was the way he showed up at his woman's home, no wonder he was in such high demand. And no wonder a rush of adrenaline jolted through her.

"And you're sure you weren't followed?" she asked, taking a step back to let him in. She figured conversation between them would distract her long enough to get her mind and body back under control.

He gave her a wry smile as he entered, moving over the threshold and filling the room the same way he'd filled the doorway…with dominating sexiness. "I'm positive. I drove around an additional twenty minutes or so to be sure. Those were good directions you gave me, by the way. I found this place without any trouble."

She nodded as she closed the door. That was when she noticed the shopping bag in his hand. When she gave him a questioning look, he said, "I made a pit stop at a store to pick up a few toiletries."

"And you weren't recognized?" she asked, moving away from the door.

"No. I had my disguise on," he said, pulling a baseball cap and a fake mustache out of the pocket of his jacket.

Rachel lifted a brow while fighting back a smile. "That's the best you can do?"

He gave her a flirty smile. "Depends on what we're talking about."

He was flirting with her.

On a few occasions over the last couple of weeks, he'd turned on the charm and flashed his devilish smile that lit up his blue-gray eyes. But she'd just rolled her eyes at him. Tonight was different. Tonight she couldn't help her body's reaction to his flirting.

As much for herself as for him, she said, "We're talking about your disguise, Ethan."

"Oh." He glanced down at the items he held in his hand. "There's nothing wrong with my disguise. It served its purpose."

With a suddenly sweaty palm, she pushed her hair behind her ear and met his gaze. "We can only hope."

Then he flashed that devilish grin that she'd tried so hard to avoid. And something slammed into her. Awareness. Attraction.

Uh-oh, said the one remaining rational part of her brain. *You've made a big mistake.*

She had to agree. Letting Ethan stay overnight just might be the biggest mistake she'd ever made.

Chapter 7

Ethan gave Rachel a hot look because there wasn't any other type of look he could give her. He was totally taken with seeing her again. Had it been just yesterday when they'd last seen each other? Just yesterday when he had been alone with her in her trailer, reclining in the chair while she applied his makeup?

She had leaned over him and her scent had almost driven him crazy. They had agreed to be just friends, and God knows he'd tried keeping his desires under control with her on the set. But at night, alone in his bed, his dreams had been another matter. She was his friend by day and his dream lover at night. And the things that went on inside those dreams were enough to make a man stiff just thinking about them.

No woman had ever dominated his thoughts like she had.

As he'd told her, he had driven around a couple of hours before finally deciding to call her. There were a number of women he could have called, but she was the one he knew he could contact and not worry about anything getting leaked to the tabloids. But now he had to be honest with himself and admit the real reason he had sought her out. He had wanted to see her.

He pulled in a deep breath, and instead of standing there staring at her like she was a nice juicy steak he couldn't wait to eat, he glanced around, needing a distraction as much as he needed a cold beer. He saw several boxes and then recalled her saying she'd only been living in this place a few months. Obviously she hadn't finished unpacking yet. But it was a nice place, large and spacious and her choice of furnishings hit the mark. "Your place is tight, Rachel."

"Thanks. You want to see the bedroom?"

At his raised brow, she said, "I mean the one you'll use tonight. The guestroom."

He'd known what she meant but thought she looked cute when she blushed. He liked seeing her get all flustered. "Sure. But you didn't ask if I wanted something to drink, and I'm thirsty."

She rolled her eyes. "Are you going to be a pesky houseguest?"

"I'll try hard not to be but I do have another confession to make. I'm hungry, too."

Rachel shook her head, chuckling. "Then you're at

the wrong place. I can give you something to drink, but for a meal you're out of luck."

"Why is that?"

"I can't cook, and before you ask, my aunt and uncle always had live-in cooks and I never had a desire to learn."

He chuckled. "No problem. I know my way around a kitchen."

She laughed. "That's all nice but there's still a problem."

"What?" he asked.

"I don't have any groceries."

He lifted a brow. "Nothing?"

"Well, my best friend did feel sorry for my refrigerator and went to the store last week and picked up a few items like eggs, butter and bread. The basics."

A smile touched his lips. "That's all I need. Just lead me to your kitchen."

"That was simply amazing," Rachel said, leaning back in her chair. "If I hadn't seen it, I would not have believed it."

Ethan leaned back in his chair as well and laughed. "It was just an egg sandwich on toast, Rachel. No big deal."

"Hey, I beg to differ. I never got the hang of cooking an egg. Or anything else for that matter."

"Why would your friend buy eggs if you can't cook them?" he asked, taking a swig of his beer. He'd found several bottles behind all the art supplies she kept in her refrigerator.

"They can be boiled, you know," she said, taking a sip of her own beer, right from the bottle. "And I know it was just a sandwich but it was still good. I hadn't realized I'd gotten hungry."

"Hadn't you eaten dinner?" he asked, getting up and grabbing their plates off the table. They had used paper plates and plastic utensils so all they had to do was trash them. No dishes to wash. How convenient. That had been a good idea on her part.

"I had lunch with my aunt and uncle earlier in the day and when I got home, I started painting and lost track of the time." She got up from the table as well. "If you hadn't called, I probably would have ordered out for a pizza or something eventually."

He watched her stride across the floor to the sink to rinse out her beer bottle before tossing it into a recycle bin. She was wearing a pair of shorts and a top and looked pretty in them. He glanced down and thought she even had cute bare feet with polished toes.

"My uncle knows you or at least he's heard of you," she said, causing him to shift his gaze to her face. "He was very complimentary."

"Was he?"

"Yes. He believes you're a person who's going places."

A broad smile touched his lips. "That means a lot coming from the likes of Jacob Wellesley," he said before finishing off his beer.

He joined her at the sink and she slid over to give him room when he proceeded to rinse out his own beer bottle. She smelled good, he thought, pulling in a whiff of her scent through his nostrils. She smelled better than good. She smelled like a woman he wanted.

He smiled over at her and she glared at him. "What's wrong?" he asked, moving to place the beer bottle in the recycle bin. "I assured you that no one followed me over here."

"That's not what's bothering me, Ethan."

He leaned back against the sink. "Then what is bothering you, Rachel?" He had an idea but wanted her to tell him.

She had moved back to the table and stood with her arms crossed over her chest. "I think we need to reiterate a few things, like the fact that two weeks ago we decided to be friends and nothing more."

"I thought we were."

"I thought so, too," she replied. "But…"

He lifted a brow and tried looking baffled. "But what?"

"I'm getting these vibes."

"Really? What kind of vibes?"

When she didn't say anything, he crossed the room to her. "Rachel, just what kind of vibes are you getting?"

He was staring at her and those gorgeous eyes of his were probably seeing a lot more than she wanted them to. A lot more than she needed them to see. And that put her on the defensive.

"None. Forget I said that," she said.

"Not sure I can do that now," he said, eyeing her up and down the way he'd done the first day they'd met. Before they'd decided all they wanted between them was friendship. Her mind scrambled as she tried to recall that day. It had been his second day on the set. Had it really been two weeks ago already? They had walked to the Disney Store and Art World. He had purchased a Princess Tiana doll for his niece, and she had picked up some art supplies.

They'd both agreed they were not involved in serious relationships and wanted to keep things that way. Besides, she had painstakingly explained to him that she didn't mix business with pleasure. He had understood and said the same rule applied to him. That should have settled things…so why didn't it?

Why was he looking at her now in a way that made her so aware of her sensuality while at the same time reminded her that it had been a long time since she'd been with a man? Nearly two years, to be exact, and even then it hadn't been anything to brag about.

"You have no choice, Ethan," she heard herself say.

"I don't?"

At the shake of her head, he said, "And what if I told you I'm getting those same vibes, and that if we don't at least share a kiss, there will always be curiosity between us?"

Heat circled around in her stomach at his admission and his suggestion. "Maybe for you, but not for me," she said, lifting her chin.

He took a step closer. "And you want me to believe that you aren't curious?"

Of course she was curious. What woman wouldn't be when there were lips that looked like his? "No, not in the least," she lied while looking him straight in the eye.

Unfortunately, those eyes were staring right back at her, as if seeing straight into her. Heat crawled all over her skin and her heart thumped faster. And when the corners of his mouth eased into a sexy smile, she inhaled sharply.

She broke eye contact with him, not liking the look on his face. It was taunting her and tempting her, all at the same time. She nervously licked her tongue across her top lip as a sudden case of panic gripped her.

God, how he'd love to try out that tongue.

Thrumming heat raced through his gut. Funny the difference a couple of weeks could make. His first days on the set, he was ready to push everything aside to focus on his role on *Paging the Doctor*. But now that he felt comfortable playing Dr. Tyrell Perry, he no longer went to bed with his lines infused into his brain. Instead something else—or should he say someone else— occupied his thoughts. And that person was standing right in front of him.

"You know what I think, Ethan?" she asked, inter- rupting his thoughts.

"No, what do you think?"

"You being here, claiming you needed a place to crash

for the night, is part of some manipulating scheme." He could hear the sharpness in her tone and could see the fire in her eyes.

"Not true. I called you for the reason I told you. I didn't have anyone else to call."

"C'mon, Ethan. Do you honestly expect me to believe that? Of all the women you've been linked to, do you really assume I'm that gullible enough to think none of them would have let you stay overnight at their place?"

"I imagine one of them would." He paused a moment and then said, "Let me rephrase what I said earlier. There are others I *could* have called but you are the only one I *wanted* to call." Boy, if only she knew how true that was.

She got silent and he knew she was thinking, trying to make heads or tails of what he'd said. Then she simply asked, "Why, Ethan? Why was I the only one you wanted to call?"

He saw the frustrated expression on her face. But it was what he saw in her eyes that captivated him. Desire. Although she might wish it wasn't there, it was and it was just as deep as what he was feeling.

But Rachel was a logical person who would not accept anything less than a logical and straightforward answer, so he said, "Because you are the only one I want."

Chapter 8

Speechless, Rachel could only stare at him while all the sexual desires she'd had for him since day one came tumbling back. Why was he trying to make things so difficult? Why was he forcing her to admit the one thing she had tried to deny? She was attracted to him something awful.

It would be so easy to let her guard down and walk across the room, wrap her arms around his neck and give in to temptation and indulge in a heated kiss. A kiss that would probably curl her toes and then some.

But she had to think logically. He threatened something she couldn't risk losing—her privacy. Any woman he was involved with would become just as much news as he was. The paparazzi would make sure of that.

He was a man who spent his life, both personal and otherwise, in front of the camera, a place she tried to avoid.

She shook her head. Things were going all wrong. They had decided they wouldn't go down this road, so why were they? They were friends and that's all they would ever be. He knew it and she knew it, as well. If he refused to do what was best, then she would.

Rachel backed up and nervously tugged at the hem of her T-shirt. "C'mon, let me show you where you'll sleep tonight. I think you'll like this room since it has its own private bath."

He held her gaze and, for a moment, she felt a weakening she didn't want to feel. Those eyes were the reason and she understood what was happening. Ethan had invaded her space, both mentally and creatively. And she couldn't deal with it.

Instead of saying anything else, she walked off and drew in a deep breath when she heard him falling in step behind her.

Walking behind her had its advantages, Ethan thought, watching the sway of Rachel's curvy hips and the lushness of her backside in her shorts. She probably hadn't figured out yet that he was enjoying the back view, and it was just as well since he definitely needed to think.

Contrary to what she thought, when he had shown up tonight it hadn't been with the intent of jumping her bones, although he found such a possibility a very enticing prospect.

He followed her up the stairs and once they reached the landing, he glanced around. The second floor was just as large and spacious as the first. There were a number of hung paintings and he couldn't help but admire them.

"Are these your creations?" he asked when she turned around after noticing he had slowed down.

She followed his gaze from wall to wall and smiled. "Some of them." She pointed out those that were. "The others are my mother's. She was a successful painter. A few of her pieces are on display at the L.A. Museum and various others."

"They're all beautiful. You inherited her gift and it shows in your work."

"Thanks."

They began walking again and as before, he followed. When she paused by a door he moved ahead and glanced inside. It was a huge room with a small bed. But it was a bed and tonight he wasn't picky, although he would much prefer hers.

"This is it," she said, entering the room. "The bath is to your left and there are plenty of towels and washcloths. Everything you need for your overnight stay."

He didn't miss her emphasis on "overnight." She intended for him to be gone in the morning. "Thanks, I appreciate it, and no matter what you think, Rachel, I didn't have an ulterior motive for coming here tonight."

Instead of saying she believed him like he'd hoped, she merely nodded, turned and walked away. Instinctively, his gaze went to her backside, and a sizzling heat began building inside of him. Hell, he was a man and tonight he was reminded of just how horny he was.

A few hours later, Rachel curled up in her favorite spot in her king-size bed. Ethan had been in her home only a few hours and already her house smelled of man. And as much as she hated admitting it, she liked the scent.

She couldn't help but notice it after rechecking the doors for the night and walking up the stairs to get ready for bed. She had heard the sound of the shower and the fragrance of his aftershave had floated through the air. Immediately, tremors of desire had rippled through her, and upon reaching the landing she had quickly hurried to her room and closed the door.

While getting dressed for bed, she had heard him moving around. The sound of someone else in her house felt strange because other than Charlene or Sofia, she rarely had houseguests.

All was quiet, so she could only assume Ethan had settled in for the night. That was just great. He was probably sleeping like a baby, and here she was, wide awake and thinking about him and the fact that he'd wanted to kiss her. She could now admit to herself—although she would never admit such a thing to him—that she had wanted to kiss him as well and that she *was* curious. However, being curious wouldn't benefit either one of them. It would serve no purpose.

Yes, it would…if it didn't lead anywhere.

Rachel rolled her eyes. *Not lead anywhere? Yeah, right.* There was no doubt in her mind that kissing Ethan would probably lead right here to her bedroom. And they had agreed to be nothing more than friends, she reminded herself.

But since he seemed quick to break the rules, why couldn't she break a few of her own? As long as the kiss and anything that followed after the kiss was all there could ever be and they knew where they stood with each other, would it really hurt for them to indulge in something that her body was telling her she both needed and wanted?

Her ears perked up when she heard the sound of Ethan moving around. A smile touched her lips. It was two in the morning and she felt grateful he couldn't sleep any more than she could.

She sat up in bed when she heard his bedroom door opening and then picked up the sound of him going downstairs. Being hungry at this hour would serve him no purpose since she didn't have any food in the house, unless he was planning to make another egg sandwich.

Before she could get cold feet, she eased out of bed, deciding if a kiss was what he wanted, then a kiss was what he was going to get.

* * *

With a deep sigh, Ethan closed the refrigerator door after pulling out a bottle of beer. He was hot and needed to cool off. He'd tried to get some sleep only to be awakened with dreams of him and Rachel together in some of the most explicit sexual positions possible. If those dreams kept coming, they could possibly ruin him for future relationships—at least until he discovered how close his dreams were to the real thing.

After screwing off the beer bottle top, he took a huge swig, appreciating how the cold liquid flowed down his throat and hoping some would keep moving straight to his groin.

"I see you couldn't sleep either."

Ethan spun around. Rachel was the last person he expected to see. After showing him the guest room, she had made herself scarce, basically hiding out in her bedroom.

She crossed the room toward the coffeepot, and he wished he could ignore the tantalizing view of her bare legs and curvy backside in a pajama set that consisted of clingy shorts and a spaghetti strap tank top.

"No, I couldn't sleep," he answered, before taking a final swig of beer while wishing it had been something stronger.

"Why?"

He looked over at her after placing his empty beer bottle on the counter. "Why what?"

"Why couldn't you sleep?" Her expression grew

troubled, showed her concern. "Isn't the bed comfortable enough?"

For a moment he thought about telling her the real deal, then decided she probably couldn't handle it if he did. "The bed is fine."

"Then what's your problem?"

He crossed his arms over his chest. "What's yours?"

Ethan hadn't meant for his tone to sound so gruff. Nor had he meant for his eyes to shift from her face to slide down to her thighs. But they did. Heat settled in his gut before he returned his gaze to her face. Just in time to see the corners of her lips lift in a wry smile. "Something amusing, Rachel?"

"You tell me." She began walking toward him and her scent—lush, exotic, jasmine and womanly—preceded her. He watched her as a sharp, tingling hunger swept through his groin, and suddenly, memories of the dream that had awakened him had his skin feeling like it was being licked with tongues of fire.

He never took her for a tease and hoped that wasn't her intent because he was not in a teasing mood. It wouldn't take much to push him over the edge right now. When she came to a stop directly in front of him, he inhaled and filled his lungs with her scent. And his testosterone level shot sky-high.

"Remember earlier when you asked me about those vibes, Ethan?" she asked.

"I remember," he said while thinking her mouth was almost too luscious for any woman's face.

"Well..."

He refused to let her get all nervous on him now. "Well what, Rachel?"

Ethan watched her take a long, slow breath. "You were right about that curiosity thing."

He didn't intend to make it easy for her. "What curiosity thing is that?"

She cleared her throat. "That curiosity thing about kissing."

He nodded slowly. "So are you admitting to being curious?"

"Umm, just a little," she said.

He went silent, deciding to let her think about what she'd said and, more importantly, what she planned to do about it.

Standing there facing Ethan, not all in his face but probably less than two feet away, Rachel concluded she had never felt anything close to the stomach-churning heat that had taken over the lower part of her body. It didn't help matters that he was shirtless with his jeans riding low on his hips. His muscular physique dominated her kitchen and reminded her that she was very much alone with a very sexy man.

And apparently he was a man who didn't forget anything, especially her evasiveness from earlier when she'd refused to elaborate on these vibes she was sensing. She was smart enough to know Ethan had no intention of letting her off the hook and was making her work for anything she got. That was fine with her, since she'd always considered herself a working girl.

He was a man who knew women. So he had to know she wanted him to kiss her. She hadn't been ready earlier tonight and hadn't been accepting. Now she was both ready and accepting. Nothing would change between them with one kiss. She was convinced of that now. Why would it? She wasn't his type and he definitely wasn't hers. Sharing a kiss wouldn't produce a marriage license or any document that said they would have to take things further than that. Monday, on the set, they would go back to being just friends. Nothing more. Nothing less.

"You think too damn hard."

She blinked upon hearing Ethan's blunt words and had to agree that she did think too hard. But then she'd always been the type of person to weigh the pros and cons before she acted. This was one of those times she had to really consider whether the pros outweighed the cons.

She quickly concluded that they did.

A smile touched her mouth when she took a couple steps closer to him, fascinated by the blue-gray eyes watching her. Now she *was* all in his face and decided it was time to do something about it. Granted, she wasn't the typical kind of woman he became involved with; however, she intended to show him that good things could come in small packages. With a pounding heart, she stood on tiptoe, reached out and placed her arms around his neck.

"Now, are we in accord?" Ethan asked, placing his hands at her waist, drawing her closer and lowering his mouth toward hers, hovering mere inches from her lips.

She drew in a deep, unsteady breath, barely able to contain the heated passion taking over her body, filling her with all kinds of sensations. She had never responded to a man this way. Had never been this affected and bold. "Yes, we're in accord."

Fueled by a degree of desire she'd never felt before, she leaned farther up on tiptoes and whispered against his lips, "So, let's go for broke."

Chapter 9

Nothing could have prepared Ethan for the need that took over his body at that moment. Unable to hold back, he captured her mouth with a possession that fueled his fire in a way it had never been with another woman. He wanted to devour Rachel alive.

A part of him couldn't believe that she was in his arms and that he was taking her mouth like it was the only feminine one left on earth. For now, for him, it was.

For some reason, he couldn't control the rush of physical hunger consuming him. His tongue tangled with hers with a voracity that sent pleasure spiking throughout his body. He was kissing her hungrily, as if he was seeking out some forbidden treat and was determined to find it.

Moments later, only because they needed to breathe, he released her mouth and stared into her stunned gaze. Refusing to allow her time to think again, he lowered his mouth once more and at the same time, he swept her off her feet and into his arms. Before the night was over, his touch would be imprinted on every inch of her skin.

Somehow he managed to get them up the stairs. Upon reaching the landing, he moved quickly toward her bedroom. She wanted to get it on and he was determined not to let anything stop them. Though he had wanted her from the first moment he'd laid eyes on her, he'd thought he would be satisfied with them just being friends. Well, he'd been proven wrong.

The moment he placed her on the bed, he joined her there, wanting to keep her in his arms, needing his lips to remain plastered to hers with his tongue inside her mouth and doing things so wicked it made his skin shiver. The kiss really had gotten ridiculously out of hand because never in his life had he been so damn greedy. So hard up to make love to a woman.

In an unexpected move, she pulled back, breaking off the kiss and drawing in a ragged breath. Her gaze latched on to the mouth that had just thoroughly kissed her, and he felt his rod pulsate when she took her tongue, that same tongue he'd tried to devour, and licked her top lip before saying, "I think we should get out of our clothes, Ethan."

He couldn't help but smile as he pulled up on his haunches. "I think you're right." He moved away from the bed to pull the jeans down his legs while flames of desire tore through him. He pulled a condom pack out of his wallet and ripped it open with his teeth. Sheathing his aroused member was an exercise in torture.

Without wasting any time, he returned to her. With a ravenous growl and a need he didn't want to question, he reached out and began removing the clothes from her body. The moment she was completely naked, the lusciousness of her feminine scent filled his nostrils and further stimulated every nerve in his body, making his protruding erection that much harder. He intended to stake a claim on every inch of her body. Beginning now.

He lowered his head and captured her mouth at the same time his hands reached around and began caressing her back and pulling her closer to the fit of him, his hard arousal pressing into her stomach.

He broke off the kiss and his mouth trailed lower, planting kisses over the soft swell of her breasts before taking a nipple into his mouth and sucking it with an intensity that made her groan.

Without losing contact with her nipple, he tilted his head and gazed up at her, saw the heated desire flaming her pupils. Returning his attention to her breasts he began kneading the other while continuing to torment the one in his mouth. He liked the feel and the taste of her and realized his desire for her was intrinsically raw.

"Ethan…"

He liked the sound of his name from her lips, and his erection throbbed mercilessly in response. "Tell me what you want, Rachel," he coaxed softly, planting kisses across her chest while his hands remained on her breasts. "Tell me what you like."

When she didn't say anything but let out a tortured groan, he blew his breath across a moist nipple. "You like that?"

She didn't hesitate, responding, "Yes."

"What about this?" he rasped in her ear before shifting, letting his wet, hot and greedy mouth slide down her body. She arched her hips the moment his mouth settled between her legs, and he could taste the honeyed sweetness of her desire on his tongue.

Her eyes were closed, her breathing was heavy. He knew she was feeling every bit of what his mouth was doing to her. With his hands he widened the opening of her legs as her taste consumed him and made him want to delve deeper into her womanly core. Her unique and sensuous flavor drove him to sample as much of her as he could get.

But he wanted to do more than that. He wouldn't be satisfied until he shattered her control the same way she had shattered his.

When he felt her body tremble beneath his mouth, he released her and pulled his body up and then over hers, easing between her legs and caging her hips with the firmness of his thighs just moments before thrusting into her. The force alone made her scream out her orgasm mere seconds before he released his.

A pulsing and fiery explosion rocked his body, which subsequently rocked hers. He leaned down and captured her mouth and knew what it felt to truly want a woman in every sense of the word.

Next time around they would go slow. And there would be a next time. He would make sure of it.

An aftermath of sensations consumed Rachel as she lay there, unable to move. Ethan excused himself to go to the bathroom, and she could barely nod in acknowledgment of what he'd said. Nor did she have the strength to turn over off her stomach and onto her back. She felt completely drained. And it wasn't because it was her first orgasm in two years. It was all about the man who'd given it to her.

Moments later, she heard him return and opened her eyes, only to see his naked body walking out of the bathroom. The dim light from the bedside lamp didn't miss his engorged erection. How could he be hard again so soon when she could barely catch her breath? And she couldn't help noticing he had on another condom. He couldn't possibly assume she had strength for another round.

The bed dipped beneath his weight as he slid in next to her. His hands began gently caressing the center of her back and the rounded curves of her buttocks. She closed her eyes again, enjoying the feel of being touched by him. When he replaced his fingers with the tip of his tongue and licked up and down her spine, a moan of pleasure escaped her lips.

Now she understood how desire could get stirred all over again so soon and gave herself up to the pure joy of it in his hands and mouth. She drew in a deep breath and then breathed out slowly, reveling in the passion building in every part of her body. It was a primitive force she didn't want to yield to again so quickly. She wanted to prolong the enjoyment.

"Turn over, baby."

She pulled in another deep breath and whispered, "Can't. Too weak."

"Then let me help you."

She heard his soft chuckle moments before he gently eased her onto her back. She stared up into his gaze, and the look in his eyes stroked something she hadn't counted on—intense desire even in her weakened state. Desire she couldn't resist or deny. She'd never wanted a man this much, so this was a first for her. And when he leaned down and claimed her mouth in a way no man had ever done before, a shiver of intense heat rode up her spine, renewing energy she didn't think she had. Her heart began pounding in her chest. At the same time, her body started shuddering with sensations she felt all the way to her toes.

With a burst of vigor that was rejuvenating every part of her, she lifted her arms and wrapped them around his neck while his mouth continued to mate with hers in a kiss that progressed from hot to scalding with a stroke of his tongue.

When he finally released her mouth it was only to shift his body between her thighs. She moaned, knowing he was about to soothe the ache at the juncture of her legs.

He reached out, cupped her bottom, lifted her hips and thrust deep inside of her. For a moment he didn't move. It was as if he needed to savor the feel of his erection planted so profoundly inside of her, pulsing, thickening and growing even larger while her inner muscles clamped down on him tightly.

Then, finally, he began moving in and out at a rhythm and pace that had every cell in her body humming, trembling and shuddering in pleasure. The muscles in his shoulders bunched beneath her fingers when he lowered his head to breathe against her mouth. Her breath hitched in her throat and then her lungs cleared in a precipitated slam.

"Ethan…"

He tasted her lips with his tongue as he drove into her. His hard thrusts made her bed shake, the springs squeak and the headboard hit against the wall. Not only was he drawing out a need and desire within her, he was fulfilling it to a degree that had her meeting him, thrust for thrust.

With one final thrust into the depth of her, her body spun into an orgasm of gigantic proportion. As she reveled in her climax, he kissed her with an intensity that elicited moans from deep in her throat.

At that moment, there was only one thing she could think of. So much for them being just friends.

* * *

Ethan eased from the bed and slipped into his jeans. Once he had snapped them up, he glanced back over his shoulder at the woman asleep in the bed. Never had any one woman touched him the way she had, in and out of bed.

And that was the crux of his problem.

He pulled in a deep breath and leaned down to brush a kiss against her temple and then quickly pulled away when he breathed in the scent of her, which had the power to render him helpless.

He rubbed a hand down his face. What the hell had he gotten himself into? Rachel had made it clear, exceedingly so and on more than one occasion, that she had no intention of getting involved with anyone she considered to be in the spotlight, anyone who would put the media on her tail. If she became involved with him, she ran the risk of that happening. He knew if there was any ounce of decency within him, he would grab his stuff and leave and when he saw her tomorrow he would pretend last night never happened.

Easier said than done.

He couldn't do that.

Something was forcing him to not only acknowledge that it happened but to do whatever he could to make sure it happened again.

He shook his head in dismay as he left the bedroom, closing the door behind him. Wasn't it just a little over two weeks ago that he'd made the vow to focus on his career more than anything else, certainly more than any woman? But there was something about Rachel that called out to him at every turn.

He had gone back into the bedroom he should have been occupying to freshen up when his cell phone on the nightstand rang. He released a deep, annoyed breath when the caller ID indicated it was his agent.

"Yes, Curtis?"

"Ethan, where are you?"

He rolled his eyes. "Is there something you need, Curtis?"

"The paparazzi can't find you."

"That's too bad," he murmured with agitation clearly in his voice. "And how did you know they were looking for me?"

His agent paused a second before saying. "It's my job to know everything that's going on with you."

Ethan frowned. Was Curtis somehow responsible for the media hounds hanging around outside of his house last night? It wouldn't surprise Ethan, since his agent liked keeping him in the news. In the spotlight, as Rachel termed it. The thought that Curtis could be connected didn't sit well with him. "Your job is to advance my career, not fabricate lies about me and my love life."

"It's never bothered you before," his agent countered.

The man was right. It hadn't bothered him before. "It does now, and it would behoove you to remember that. Talk to you later, Curtis."

Ethan then disconnected the call.

* * *

The sound of a ringing telephone worked its way into the deep recesses of Rachel's sleep-shrouded mind. Without lifting her head from the pillow, she reached out and grabbed her cell phone off the bedside table. "Hello," she said in a drowsy voice.

"I can't believe you're still in bed."

Rachel forced one eye open upon hearing her sister's voice. "What time is it?"

"Almost noon. You weren't at church today, and Aunt Lily wanted to make sure you were okay since it's not like you to miss service."

Rachel moaned, which was followed by a deep yawn. "I'm fine, Sofia." *Am I really?* "I overslept." That wasn't a lie.

She slowly pulled herself up in bed, surprised she had the energy to do so. Taking part in lovemaking marathons wasn't something she did often, and thanks to Ethan, her muscles had gotten one heck of a workout.

Ethan…

She glanced at the rumpled spot beside her in the bed. It hadn't been a figment of her imagination. He had been there. His masculine scent was still in her bedcovers. And she could hear him moving around downstairs, which meant he was still there.

She closed her eyes as memories of their lovemaking flowed through her mind. There were the memories of his hands all over her body, his tongue licking her nipple, his head between her legs, his—

"Rachel?"

She snapped her eyes back open. "Yes?"

"I asked if you wanted to do a movie later."

Sofia was a workaholic and any other time Rachel would have jumped at the chance to do something fun with her sister, but not today. But she knew better than to tell her sister the real reason. "Can I get a rain check? I want to finish this painting so it can be ready for the gallery's opening day."

"Sure, just let me know when."

They talked for a few more minutes and then Sofia had to take another call. Rachel disconnected the call and stretched her body in bed, thinking that as much as she had enjoyed making love with Ethan, it couldn't happen again.

She eased out of bed, knowing they needed to talk.

Few people knew that cooking was one of Ethan's favorite pastimes, so he wasn't taken aback by the look of surprise on Rachel's face when she walked into her kitchen. Her sexy-pixie expression was priceless.

Something else that was priceless was the way she was dressed. She had showered and was wearing a printed sundress with spaghetti straps at the shoulders and a cute pair of sandals on her feet. On anyone else the simple outfit would have been so-so, but not on her. It gave her an "at-home" look that couldn't be captured any day on the set.

There were a number of reasons for him to make that conclusion. Heading the list was the fact that this was the first time he'd seen her out of bed since they'd made love, so in his book she could have worn a gunnysack and she still would have looked good to him.

"Ethan, what are you doing?" she asked, glancing around her kitchen.

"I'm preparing brunch. I figured you'd be hungry when you finally woke up." He didn't have to say why he'd expected her to sleep late. Last night had been quite a night for them. He doubted either of them had gotten a full hour's sleep.

"But where did you find the stuff to prepare this spread?"

He smiled. "I went to that grocery store on the corner, and before you ask, no, I wasn't recognized. I wore my disguise and quickly went in and out."

"But your car…"

"I drove yours." At the lift of her brow he said, "I left a note just in case you woke up while I was gone."

"Oh." The thought of his male scent infusing the interior of her car was almost too much to think about. Now she would drive her car and think about him.

"You like cooking, I gather," she said moving across the room to the coffeepot. The coffee smelled good but she smelled even better. There was a sensuality to her fragrance that could reach him on a masculine level each and every time he took a whiff of her.

He chuckled. "You gathered right, although I didn't get an interest until college. It was a quick and easy way to get a girl up to your dorm room."

She glanced at him over her shoulder. "I'm sure getting a girl up to your room wasn't hard, Ethan."

A grin formed on his lips. "Should I take that as a compliment?"

"You should take it for whatever you want. I know it to be true. Most women would find you simply irresistible."

He tilted his head and looked at her. She was reaching up to open one of the cabinet doors, which was an almost impossible feat for her without stretching and standing on tiptoes. What flashed through his mind at that moment was a reminder of a position they had used last night when they'd made love standing up. Those same feet had been wrapped around him, locking him inside her body. "Do you find me irresistible, Rachel?"

She turned around to face him, leaning back against the kitchen counter as she did so. Her gaze roamed over him, up and down, before coming to settle on his face where she gave him her full attention. His stomach tightened at her perusal since it seemed as intimate as any physical caress could get. She pushed a few strands of hair behind her ear before a smile touched her lips. It was tantalizing in one sense but frightening in another.

"Yes, but not the same way that other women do."

Her words, spoken both seriously and honestly, had a profound effect because a part of him knew they were true. She had a way of seeing beyond what the media described as the "killer-watt" smile, past the persona of a jaw-dropping Hollywood leading man. In the two weeks they'd known each other, she'd shown him that she had the ability to get to know the real Ethan Chambers. She knew that what you saw was not always what you got.

And that made *her* irresistible.

Needing to touch her, wanting to kiss her, especially at that moment, he moved toward her and pulled her into his arms. She came willingly, without preamble, filled with all the grace and refinement that most women didn't possess. She had the ability to change the physical to the sensual the moment her lips locked with his. She also had the intuition to know that when it came to an attraction between them, he needed more.

And more importantly, she was willing to give it.

He pulled her closer, wanting to seal every inch of space between them. She leaned up, wrapped her arms around his neck and tilted her head back automatically to meet his mouth that came swooping down on hers. He needed her in the way a man needed a woman.

A woman he was beginning to think of as his.

Nobody kisses like Ethan Chambers, Rachel concluded when she could manage to think again. She loved being held captive in his strong grip, loved being the recipient of his lusty and marauding tongue. And she loved the feel of her breasts pressed against the hard and firm lines of his chest. The same chest she had kissed every inch of last night. Even then she had felt the strength of it beneath her lips. Ethan had a body that was an artist's dream, and she would love to paint him one day, capture the essence of all his masculine beauty on canvas.

"Brunch has to wait."

Those words were barely out of his mouth before he swept her off her feet and into his arms. Once again she had managed to drive him out of control and she enjoyed every single moment of doing so. It was only last night that she had discovered her ability as a woman and the pleasure-filled places that skill could take her.

It might have been his intent to take her back to bed, but somewhere between the kitchen and living room he decided they couldn't make it that far. He headed for her sofa.

Her heart began beating rapidly because with Ethan she had discovered you never knew what you would get, but the one thing you could expect was the most intense pleasure any man could deliver. And that knowledge caused an intense ache between her legs that only he could appease.

She caught her breath when she felt the sofa cushion touch her back, and he spread her out as if she was a sampling for his enjoyment. He would soon discover that he was also one for hers. His musky and ultrasexy scent was devouring all common sense in her body and replacing it with a spine-tingling need that had her moaning out his name.

"I'm right here, baby," he whispered while quickly removing the clothes from her body and then from his. When he stood over her naked, fully aroused and looking as handsome as any man had a right to look, she was filled with a craving that had her moving upward, launching herself at him and toppling them both to the floor.

He cushioned their fall, and they ended up with their legs entangled and her stretched out over him. Just the way she wanted. Some deep, dark emotion, an intense hunger he had tapped into last night, consumed her and she began licking him all over, starting with his broad shoulders and working her way downward.

Moving past his tight abs, she cupped his erection in her hands before lowering her head and taking him fully, needing the taste, texture and total length of him between her lips and as deep in her mouth as he could go.

"Rachel!"

His palms bracketed her head, his fingers dug into her scalp and his moan became music to her ears while she proceeded to torture him. She felt his shaft swell deep inside her mouth and she stretched to accommodate its size.

"I'm coming, baby."

And he did.

She appeased every deep craving she ever had, using her throat to prolong his orgasm. He seemed lost, powerless as he gave himself over to the magic she created. And she reveled in the control as she never had before.

When he could draw another breath, he pulled a condom pack from his jeans, sheathed himself and entered her. Quick work but thorough.

He began moving in and out of her, thrusting hard

and deep, taking her to the brink where she'd led him moments ago. No matter what would come tomorrow, she knew she would have these memories of their lovemaking. Memories that would comfort her and tear at her heart long after he was no longer a part of her life.

But for now, for today, he was and because of that, she was satisfied.

It was time for him to leave.

After making love on her living room floor, they had returned to the kitchen and eaten the brunch he had prepared before going back up to her bedroom and making love some more. When they were spent, they had showered together, returned downstairs to devour the apple tarts he'd made for dessert, then he'd gone upstairs to gather his few belongings.

"Do you think the paparazzi have gone now?" she asked, walking him to the kitchen door that led to her garage where his car was parked beside hers.

"Yes. I spoke with the manager of my condo complex and she apologized profusely. The one thing I was assured of when I moved in was that my privacy would be protected. She doesn't understand what could have happened." He paused. "I think I do."

She lifted a brow. "What?"

"My agent. He thinks one of the ways to build my career is for me to stay in the spotlight, to keep my name in the news."

He could tell her mind was at work. Making that

statement had made her remember her one argument as to why there could never be anything but friendship between them. For that reason, he was not surprised by her next statement.

"I refuse to think of this weekend as a mistake, Ethan, but it's something we can't allow to happen again. You are who you are and I am who I am. We live different lives and reside in basically different worlds."

"It doesn't have to be that way, Rachel."

"Yes, it does. I could never ask you to give up your dream for me, like you can't expect me to do the same for you."

He paused for a moment and then asked, "So where do we go from here?"

A sad smile touched her lips. "Nowhere. Let's chalk it up as nothing more than a one-night stand. This weekend is our secret. And it's up to us to know it was just one of those things that can't happen again."

He glanced down as if studying the floor and then he looked back at her. "What if I said I don't agree? That there has to be a way?"

A bittersweet smile touched her lips. "Then I'd say don't waste your time trying to figure one out. It doesn't exist. We are as different as day and night."

Ethan pulled in a deep breath and felt a tightening in his gut because he knew, in a way, she was right. Becoming a successful Hollywood actor was his dream, and it was a dream that didn't mesh with hers.

He leaned down and kissed her hard and deep. Only one thought pierced his mind then and again moments later when he walked out her door. How on earth was he going to give her up?

Chapter 10

"Quiet on the set!
"Take three!
"Action!"

Rachel could hear the sound of Frasier's booming voice carrying all the way into her trailer. Today they would be shooting mostly medical scenes, and several doctors from an area hospital were on the set to make sure that aspect of the show was done correctly.

She had arrived at work early, mainly to have herself together by the time Ethan got there. Like she'd told him yesterday, although she hadn't regretted any of it, their time together could not be repeated. For twenty-four hours she had let herself go and had made love to a man who had pleasured her body in ways probably not known to most men. All women should be made love to the way Ethan had done to her. Memories of their time together still made her skin hot whenever she thought about it.

When he had arrived this morning, he had not given her any more of his time and attention than he always had. There was no way anyone seeing them interact together would suspect they'd spent practically the entire weekend behind closed doors. There had been so much red-hot chemistry between them and they had taken advantage of it time and time again.

Although no one on the set had a clue, each and every time he glanced her way or gave her a smile, heat would begin simmering in the pit of her stomach. One look into Ethan's eyes had the power to send a rush of desire spiking through her. That was why she was letting Theresa work out on the set today, brushing up the actors during shooting, while she remained in her trailer applying the makeup for those in the next scene.

"You're quiet today."

Rachel blinked, remembering where she was and what she was doing. There never had been a time when thoughts of a man had interfered with her job. She looked down at Tae'Shawna Miller, the model-turned-actress from last season who played a nurse on the show. Tae'Shawna was known to be moody and self-centered and, not surprisingly, months ago she'd begun hanging around Paige.

Rachel wasn't sure what Paige might have told her,

but lately Tae'Shawna had been acting even moodier where she was concerned. She'd even gone to John saying Rachel had applied her makeup too heavily last season and that she wanted to bring in her own makeup artist. John had denied her request.

"It's Monday," Rachel said, hoping that would end things. It was a joke on the set that although Wednesday was considered hump day, Monday was pretty low-key with everyone trying to recover from the weekend.

"I hear you, girl. I could barely pull myself out of bed. If it wasn't for Ethan calling to wake me up this morning, I probably would have been late coming in today."

Trying to keep her hands steady and acting as nonchalant as she could, Rachel continued applying Tae'Shawna's makeup and asked in a casual tone, "Ethan Chambers?"

A smile touched the woman's lips. "None other. We spent some time together this weekend. I'm only mentioning this to you because I know you're the soul of discretion. Ethan would be upset if he knew I told anyone. He wants to keep things quiet since we're both working on the show."

The woman gave a naughty smile before adding, "Needless to say, I had to all but force him to leave last night."

Rachel managed to remain calm as she dissected the woman's words, hoping what Tae'Shawna was saying was more wishful thinking than gospel truth, especially since Ethan had been with *her* from Saturday night to late yesterday afternoon.

But she couldn't help wondering if he had left her bed and gone directly to Tae'Shawna's. And where had he been before coming to her place on Saturday night? She'd felt it hadn't been her place to ask. However, now the woman in her couldn't help wondering if Ethan had shared his weekend with her *and* Tae'Shawna.

That question was still on her mind hours later. For the moment, her trailer was empty and she slid into the chair to take a breather, trying to fight the green-eyed monster of jealousy consuming her. She pulled in a deep breath, wondering why the thought of Ethan being involved with Tae'Shawna bothered her and how she could get beyond it.

The odds had been high when he'd shown up at her place Saturday night that he would probably spend some of his weekend with another woman. It would have made perfect sense that he did. After all, he was a known playboy around town. It really shouldn't concern her since they had used protection every time they'd made love, so she wasn't at risk. But still…

It disappointed her that, on the set, Ethan portrayed himself as a man not giving any of the women who came on to him the time of day. Although he was always friendly to them, she'd had no reason to assume that things had been any different after hours. Was it only an act? Was he involved not only with Tae'Shawna but others as well, possibly even Paige?

She eased from the chair and began pacing. She told

herself she should not be bothered if he was also seeing other women. They hadn't set any rules or guidelines regarding their relationship. A frown deepened her brow when she reminded herself they didn't have a relationship. What happened this weekend was just a one-time deal. She had made that clear to Ethan. But why had he bothered to make it seem as if he hadn't had sex for a while, certainly not that same day? Men!

She knew when it came to sex, men would get as much of it as came their way and still want more. A part of her couldn't help feeling somewhat disappointed to discover he was one of those men and wasn't different at all.

"Looks like you're thinking too hard again."

She spun around to find the object of her deepest and most disappointing thoughts leaning against the trailer door. She hadn't heard him enter the trailer.

"And what's it to you?" she asked in a tone that sounded pretty snippy to even her own ears.

He shrugged. "With that attitude, nothing, I guess. Frasier gave everyone an additional hour for lunch again, and I was wondering if you'd like to take a walk over to—"

"No." And then because she knew there was no reason for her to have an attitude, she said, "Thanks for asking, but I have a lot to do here."

He nodded slowly as he continued to look at her. She wished he wouldn't do that. And she wished it didn't bother her, didn't make her feel those vibes again, especially when he probably looked at Tae'Shawna the same way. Not only Tae'Shawna but all the other women with whom he was probably involved.

"Is that why you haven't been out on the set today?"

"You could say that."

Avoiding his gaze, she moved around the trailer, picking up items to repack in her various makeup kits, as well as hanging up items of clothing that cast members had discarded.

"Is something wrong, Rachel?"

She glanced over at him. "No. What gives you that idea?" She then returned to what she was doing, basically presenting her back to him.

Moving away from the door, Ethan strode through the space separating them and came to stand in front of her, forcing her to look up and meet his gaze. "Hey, I knew yesterday you were serious about continuing this 'friends only' thing and, although I prefer more between us, I will respect your wishes."

"Do you?"

He had a confused look on his face. "Do I what?" His tone was low, gruff, with more than a hint of agitation.

"Do you prefer more between us?"

He released a frustrated sigh. "I told you I did."

She nodded slowly. "And what did you tell Tae'Shawna?" The moment the words left her lips, she wished she could take them back. She probably sounded like a jealous shrew. And she had no right to be that way, considering she had told Ethan there would be nothing between them. Ever.

She stared up at him to see even more confusion settle in his features when he asked, "Is this supposed to be a trick question or something?"

"Not a trick question, Ethan, just a curious one."

He crossed his arms over his chest. "And what does Tae'Shawna have to do with us?"

A shiver ran through her when he said the word *us.* Although when it came to them there was no "us," just hearing him say it did something crazy to her. "By 'us,' you mean you and Tae'Shawna?" she asked.

A smile that didn't quite reach his eyes touched his lips. "Was that question supposed to be a joke, Rachel?"

"What do you think?" She made a move to walk away but he reached out and gripped her arm, not too tight, but enough that the heat of his hand felt like a flame licking her skin. *Amazing,* she thought. Even when she wasn't happy with him, he had the ability to make her want him.

"Explain what you meant by that," he said. She thought she heard somewhat of a growl in his tone.

He was staring at her, and she returned his stare with no intention of breaking it. And she had no problem explaining what she'd said as well as elaborating on what she'd meant. "When I worked on Tae'Shawna's makeup earlier today, she took me into her confidence and shared information about you and her."

His expression seemed thoughtful. "Me and her?"

"Yes."

"And what did she say?"

She shrugged and then said, "Nothing more than that the two of you spent part of the weekend together and that you didn't leave her place until late last night and that you were her wake-up call this morning. I know you were with me from Saturday night until yesterday afternoon, but—"

"You're not sure about the time I wasn't with you?" he said, finishing her statement for her.

"Yes, but it really doesn't matter. Saturday night just happened between us. And it's not like I didn't know about your reputation."

He nodded as he held her gaze. "My reputation that you know about from a tabloid you *don't* read. Right?"

It was easy to see his expression had gone from thoughtful to rigid, as if he was struggling to contain the anger she could actually feel radiating from him. She was smart enough to take a step back when he took one forward, and she noticed the eyes staring at her had turned a stormy gray. Not a good sign.

She took another step backward only to have her spine hit a wall. He caged her in when he leaned forward, bracing his hands against the wall on both sides of her face. If his aim was to get her attention, he had it.

She lifted her chin and met his glare with one of her own. "What is this about, Ethan?"

"You tell me, Rachel."

"I told you. And I also told you that you don't owe me an explanation about Tae'Shawna because—"

"I wouldn't repeat it if I were you," he interrupted in a tone gruff enough to make her heed his warning.

He didn't say anything for a moment. He just stared at her. Then finally he said, "First of all, when I made love to you Saturday night, it was the first time I had been intimate with a woman in over six months."

She couldn't stop her mouth from dropping open. Nor could she disguise the flicker of surprise in her eyes. Both were probably what made him continue on to say, "This weekend I needed to get away, so I got up early Saturday morning and drove across the border to Tijuana. Alone. When I got back later that night, I discovered the paparazzi camped out at my place and called you. When I left your apartment Sunday afternoon, I went straight home. I don't know what make-believe game Tae'Shawna is playing but, unfortunately, it's not the first time and probably won't be the last time that some woman claimed we were together or involved in an affair when we weren't. That's how those tabloids you *don't* read are sold."

"Ethan, I—"

His sharp tone interrupted her. "The only thing I want to know from you now is whether you believe me or Tae'Shawna."

She frowned. "Does it matter?"

"To me it does."

She took a deep, uneven breath as she stared into his eyes, still jarred by his admission that their night together had been his first time in over six months. Her heart was pounding because he indicated what she believed mattered to him. And although she didn't quite understand why, she was glad that it did.

As odd as it might seem, she didn't want him to be involved with women like Tae'Shawna, women who would go so far as to invent a relationship with a man. Or even worse, women like Paige who would try anything to get him into their beds.

There was one thing that was actually making her feel somewhat warm inside—the fact that he hadn't wanted any of the model types. He had wanted her. And the strangest thing of all was that she didn't want any of those other women to have him either.

She couldn't explain the thought processes that supported her reasons, especially not to him when they were still somewhat foggy to her. But what she could do was give him the answer he was still waiting for. "I don't believe you're involved with Tae'Shawna, Ethan."

Ethan hadn't realized he was holding his breath until he released it after Rachel had spoken. Why what she believed mattered so much he wasn't sure, but it did. It might have everything to do with that bond he felt with her. A bond he'd never felt with any other woman. That bond had strengthened when they'd made love. He wondered if she realized it. If she didn't comprehend it now, he was certain she would later.

Needing to kiss her, he reached out and pulled her into his arms and captured her mouth with his. All the reasons this weekend had meant so much to him came roaring back to life like a living thing with a mind of its own. It had the ability to push him closer to her even when she wanted to keep him at a distance.

He tried to steady his heart rate and had almost succeeded until she wrapped her arms around his neck and pressed her body closer to his while returning his kiss with equal fervor. Her response was what he had hoped for and definitely what he was enjoying. It wouldn't take much for him to take her like this, standing up against the wall. He fought the temptation. Instead, he continued to make love to her mouth with a hunger that seemed relentless. The feel of her hardened nipples pressing against his chest was sweet agony, as was the rough texture of her denim jeans rubbing against his hard erection. He continued to fight the temptation, knowing what his body wanted would only lead to trouble.

That fight was taken out of his hands when they heard the sound of conversation right outside the trailer door and they quickly ended the kiss. He took a deep breath while forcing his body to cool down, which seemed nearly impossible to do.

He reached out and flicked the pad of his thumb across her bottom lip. "I know what you said last night, but I think we'll be doing each other an injustice not to explore what could be, Rachel. There will be risks but I intend to convince you they will be worth it."

He leaned down and swiped a quick kiss across her lips before moving toward the door.

Chapter 11

"Let me make sure I got this right." Wide-eyed, Charlene spoke in a low tone of voice as she leaned across the table while they waited in Roscoe's for their food to be served. Lower still, she said, "You spent the weekend with Mr. Drop-Dead Gorgeous himself? Ethan Chambers?"

At least Charlene hadn't blurted it out in a loud voice, Rachel thought, grateful for that, although it was evident Charlene was stunned. "Only *part* of the weekend," she quickly clarified. "He arrived around eight Saturday night and left Sunday afternoon around five. That's not even a full twenty-four hours." What she didn't have to say, and what Charlene could figure out on her own, was that a lot had happened during that period of time.

"Wow!" Charlene said, still clearly stunned. "Two weeks ago you said the two of you were nothing more than friends. What happened?"

Rachel drew in a deep breath, wondering how she was going to explain to her best friend that lust happened. The man was simply irresistible, both in and out of bed. "Well, it happened like this…"

Charlene leaned even farther over the table. Not only were her ears perked but her eyes were bright with curiosity. Rachel figured she was more than ready to take in all the hot-tamale details. "Yes?"

When Rachel didn't say anything, Charlene lifted a brow. "Well?"

A smile touched Rachel's lips. "Well what?"

Charlene gave her a don't-you-dare-play-with-me-like-that look. "Tell me what happened."

"Whatever you can imagine probably did happen, Cha. The man knew positions that are probably outlawed in most states, and he has more staying power in bed than Peyton Manning has on a football field."

A huge grin lit Charlene's face as she sat back in her chair. She exclaimed proudly as she looked at her with envy, "What a woman."

Rachel shook her head as she recalled the past weekend. "No, what a man."

And she seriously meant that. Ethan had her considering taking risks she normally would not take. He said he would make it worth her while and, considering this past weekend, she had no reason not to believe him. After that incident in the trailer a few days ago, she had been trying to keep a level head around the set and handle things decently and in order. In other words, although she didn't try to avoid him, she didn't do anything to seek him out either. But she was well aware that he was waiting for her to make the next move.

She glanced over at Charlene. "What have I gotten myself into?"

Charlene smiled naughtily. "His pants, for starters."

"Girl, be serious," Rachel protested.

"I am."

Rachel chuckled. Yes, her friend was serious and also right. She had gotten into his pants and was looking forward to getting into them again. How shameful was that?

"It doesn't make sense," she said. "You know what a private person I am and how I hate being in the spotlight. Anyone involved with Ethan will have their face plastered all over the tabloids. There's no way to get around that unless we sneak around."

"And how do you feel about doing something like that?"

That was a good question and one she needed to think about. Were earth-shattering, toe-curling orgasms worth all of that?

"You know what's wrong with you, don't you?" Charlene asked, smothering a giggle.

Rachel took a sip of her iced tea. "I don't have a clue."

"You went without a hot male body too long. Trust me, I know how it feels."

Rachel hated to admit that Charlene was probably right. In the past, she'd always had enough on her plate to keep her mind occupied so she didn't think about sex. She was just as busy now as she was before, so what was there about Ethan that made her want to make him a top priority on her "to do" list? It wasn't like she wasn't routinely surrounded on the set by gorgeous, sexy men. Why had her body decided Ethan was the one?

Before she could offer any more input to the conversation, her cell phone began vibrating. Caller ID indicated an unknown number. Normally she refused to answer those kinds of calls, but she felt a warm sensation in the pit of her stomach. She excused herself from the table and quickly headed toward the ladies' room.

"Yes?"

"This is Ethan. I want to see you."

So much for him waiting for her to make the next move.

The sound of his voice plunged her into a sea of desire so deep she felt herself going under. "Why? Do I need to save you again?"

"No, but I do need you to make love to me like you did last weekend."

If she hadn't been drowning before, she was certainly drowning now and there was no one around to throw her a life jacket.

"Ethan, I think—"

"You do too much of that."

For a moment she struggled with the possibility that maybe he was right. "One of us needs to."

"No, we don't. Just consider it something we both deserve. We work hard, so we should get to play harder."

He did have a point. Didn't he?

She drew in a deep breath, wondering where her logical mind was when she needed it the most. It had probably taken a flying leap with that first orgasm Saturday night. "We're risking the chance of you being followed."

"I have everything under control."

Including her, she thought, when she tried summoning the gumption to deny what he was asking. But then all she had to do was to remember Saturday night or the kiss they'd shared in her trailer earlier in the week. His lips had teased her mercilessly, and his tongue had nearly made her short-circuit.

"Rachel?"

"Yes?"

"Will you meet me?"

She nervously licked her lips. "Where?"

He rattled off an address that was followed by a brief set of instructions. "Do you need directions?"

"No, I'll use my GPS," she said, tucking the piece of paper she'd written on back in her purse.

Moments later, she hung up the phone with her heart pounding in her chest. Emotions she refused to put a name to stirred in her stomach, and she knew she was falling deeper and deeper into lust.

* * *

Slow down, buddy. The last thing you need is a ticket while racing across town for a night of hot and heavy sex.

Ethan flinched at the thought of that because he knew his meeting with Rachel was more than that. She was different and not just because she wasn't a woman anxious to blast their affair to all who'd listen.

And they were involved in an affair because neither of them was looking for any sort of heavy-duty relationship right now. He was satisfied to keep things under wraps as much she was, especially since he knew how she felt about the matter.

He had actually been followed for a short while after leaving his place. He had driven his car to the private parking garage of condos owned by a friend of Hunter's from college. If the person tailing him thought he was smart, Ethan intended to show he was smarter.

Ethan had parked his car in a designated spot and had donned his disguise before getting out of his car and getting into another vehicle—one owned by that same friend of Hunter's who was presently out of the country for the next month or so.

He had smiled upon leaving the garage and bypassing the photographer who was parked across the street, waiting for Ethan to come out. No doubt, the man would be there for some time while trying to determine what woman and at what address Ethan was visiting at this particular condo complex.

Ethan couldn't ever recall going through this much

hassle to keep his interest in a woman hidden. If he wasn't so concerned about Rachel's feelings, he truly wouldn't give a damn.

But he needed tonight. He needed her. This had been one hell of a week, with Frasier in rare form, demanding more than perfection from everyone. The rumor floating around the set was that the man and his partner were having problems. Although Frasier's policy demanded all of them leave any and all personal matters at the door and not bring them on the set, evidently that rule didn't apply to Frasier.

Luckily, so far none of Frasier's tirades had been leveled at him but at a number of others, including Tae'Shawna when she had messed up her lines. After the lie she'd told to Rachel, the woman hadn't gotten any pity from Ethan.

He had come close to confronting Tae'Shawna on more than one occasion about the lie she had told. However, Rachel had asked him not to say anything. She worried that Tae'Shawna would resent her for breaking a confidence and possibly even retaliate in some way.

Ethan exited off the interstate and noted a lot of cars on the road for a Thursday night. He was in Industry, a city in the San Gabriel Valley section of Los Angeles. His destination was an old warehouse owned by Chambers Winery that was used to store bottled wine shipped from the vineyard. In other words, it used to be their off-site wine cellar. More than once he had considered the idea of fixing up at least part of the place as a possible hideaway when he needed peace from the media's scrutiny. This week he had acted on that idea, and after a few phone calls and explicit instructions, he had received word that the place was good to go. He couldn't imagine not bringing Rachel here to help christen the place.

More than once during the drive over, he had glanced back in his rearview mirror to make sure he was not being followed. Satisfied that he had not been, he pulled into the drive and around the side of the building that was away from the street.

Grabbing the pair of wine glasses off the seat beside him, he got out of the car and closed the door behind him. It was a beautiful August night with bright stars lighting the sky. The perfect night for a romantic rendezvous.

He had made good time, intentionally arriving ahead of Rachel. As he headed for the entrance with the wine glasses in his hands, he smiled. So far so good. His evening was going according to his plans.

Rachel pulled into the parking lot of the huge vacant building to park next to the vehicle already there. Her heart began pounding and her hand on the steering wheel began trembling somewhat.

She glanced around through her windshield. She had followed Ethan's instructions to the letter, and the huge building looming before her appeared dark and scary. But she knew somewhere inside, Ethan was waiting for her.

She opened the car door and glanced around as she

got out. It had been hard for her to consume her dinner knowing what her plans were for afterward.

If Charlene suspected anything was amiss, she hadn't let on. Rachel would give her best friend all the details later. But for now, the plan for tonight was something she hadn't wanted to share. She didn't want to take the risk of anyone talking her out of doing something she really wanted to do. She didn't want anyone to knock the craziness out of her and force her to go back to being her logical self.

She pushed the door and, to her intense relief, it opened, just like Ethan had said it would. The moment she stepped over the threshold, the smell of vintage wine consumed her nostrils. She could probably get intoxicated just from the scent alone.

The place was dark. The only light was a bit of moonlight shining in through one of the windows. She'd never been afraid of the dark but there was something eerie about this place. Her heart rate increased, and she fought back a nervousness that was about to consume her as she took a step back and bumped against the hard, solid wall of a masculine chest.

She gasped when a pair of strong, muscular arms reached around to enclose her within a powerful embrace. The familiar scent of him surrounded her and she breathed it in and relaxed against him. She could feel his hot breath at her neck, close to ear, when he whispered, "Welcome to my lair."

Her heart rate steadied when another type of response took control—not fear of the unknown but apprehension of the known. She knew why she was here, why he had asked her to come and how tonight would end up.

She released her breath with a shaky sigh when he turned her to face him and leaned forward to give her a more physical display of welcome, one she had no problem receiving.

His tongue tangled hotly with hers while his hands seemed to roam all over her, finding her bare skin not covered by her short skirt. And he was caressing her backside in a way that only he could execute. When he finally pulled back, she was grateful for his hands around her waist because her knees seemed to buckle beneath her, and she felt herself swaying against him.

He held her tight as he continued to rain kisses all over her face while his hands gently massaged her back. They stood that way for a while as their heartbeats and breathing returned to normal. But she was completely aware of the way her hard nipples pressed against the hard wall of his chest.

"Come on, let me show you around," he whispered against her temple.

He took her hand in his, and using a flashlight that he pulled from his pocket, he led the way. She glanced from side to side and saw rows and rows of wine bottles and immediately knew this was a place his family owned.

"There's usually a security guard around," he said. "Clyde has worked for us at this place for years, making sure no one runs off with anything. I thought I'd give him the rest of the night off."

Instead of saying anything, Rachel nodded and

merely followed him through another door and up a flight of stairs. She tried pushing back the question rushing through her mind. Why was she here and not at home in her own bed getting a good night's sleep? After all, it was Thursday and tomorrow was a workday for the both of them. But she knew the reason. Ethan had called and said he wanted them to make love again. She wanted them to make love again as well. For what other reason would she be here?

She knew getting involved with him, secretly or otherwise, was probably not a good idea, but then she could do casual dating just like the next man or woman. She wasn't looking for everlasting love. She liked her life just fine the way it was.

He used a key to open another door and it was only then that he put the flashlight away and flipped on a switch. She nearly closed her eyes at the brightness but not before she saw the immaculate-looking office.

She continued to glance around when he locked the door behind them. And when she gave him a questioning look, he smiled before taking her hand again and leading her through another set of doors.

She gasped when she saw what was in front of her. It was the most beautifully decorated room she could imagine, one designed as a lovers' hideaway, complete with a king-size bed and all the other matching furnishings. There was even an expensive throw rug on the floor and several beautiful paintings on the wall, lit candles around the room and a vase of roses sitting on a dresser.

She lowered her head when an errant thought hit her. Was this where Ethan brought all his conquests when he needed privacy? She glanced over at him and apparently the question was there, looming in her gaze, because he said, "I called and had this place renovated just a few days ago. I'm pleased with what they've done in such a short period of time."

And then in a voice that had thickened, taken on a rough edge in an ultrasexy sort of way, he said, "And let me go on record as saying that you're the only woman I've ever brought here, Rachel. I consider this place as ours."

Her breath caught in her throat as she took in all he said and all he meant. He had created this place for them? Did he assume there would be many more secret rendezvous for them? So many that they would need a place to slip away to and be together without prying eyes or stalking photographers hell-bent on fueling the tabloid frenzy?

The thought of such an idea—Ethan being so into her—was ludicrous. She could see him taking advantage of her willingness to engage in no-strings-attached sex a couple of times, but did he honestly think it would become a long-term affair? No, he probably knew that it wouldn't be and would be satisfied with the here and now. When she ceased being his flavor of the hour, he would replace her with someone else, someone more his style. More than likely it would be one of those leggy models his name was usually hooked up with. A woman who enjoyed being in the spotlight just as much as he did.

She fought the thick lump blocking her throat. Not wanting to put a damper on the mood he'd set for them tonight, she let her eyes roam around the room. The decor was simply beautiful in the warm glow of candlelight. Then her eyes lit on the glasses and the bottle of wine on a nightstand beside the bed.

"That's Chambers Winery's finest," he leaned over and whispered close to her ear. She glanced up into the depths of his eyes, saw all the desire embedded deep within them, and an unfamiliar sensation overtook her. It ran through her like a burning ball of heat and settled in the pit of her stomach as if it belonged there and had no intention of going away.

Mentally she weighed her options. She could take tonight and accept it for what it was—a night two sexually charged individuals wanted to enjoy each other. Or she could go along for the ride as long as it lasted and as long as they took all the measures necessary not to get caught—providing it was all enjoyment and no emotion. There *had* to be a no-emotional-attachment policy.

Deciding which option she would go with, she eased closer to him and said, "I can't wait to have a glass."

The tips of her nipples were beginning to heat up, and she intentionally rubbed against him to bring her breasts in contact with his chest. The hitch in his breath let her know she'd made a hit. It seemed Hollywood's newest heartthrob wasn't immune to her charms. Just the thought that she had enough to hold his interest made her heart pound and her entire body begin to tremble inside.

The look in his eyes told her that he knew exactly what she was doing and was willing to let her take the lead for now.

"And there's something else I can't wait to have," she said, tilting her head back to meet his gaze.

"What else do you want, Rachel?"

The huskiness of his voice made a shiver ripple through her. She lowered her gaze to his chest and then lower still to his crotch. She'd never been fascinated with the makings of an aroused man before, but now she couldn't help marveling at what a fine specimen of a man he was. His erection nearly burst through the zipper of his jeans, and she felt proud of herself that she had caused his intense arousal.

"I want this," she said, reaching out and groping that part of him. She heard his low growl and glanced up. His eyes could not hide the desire she saw in them.

"Sweetheart, I'm going to make sure you get everything you want." And then he swept her off her feet and into his arms and carried her over to the bed.

There was something about Rachel's scent that got to him every time. It was an intimate fragrance that seemed to beckon him on a primitive level that even now had every muscle in his body rippling in a way he found tormenting.

He undressed her and then undressed himself. He

had seen the way she blushed when he tossed several condom packets on the nightstand and took a step away from the bed to put one on. She watched him sheath himself and the thought that she was doing so sent a rush of blood to his loins.

Silence dominated the room and for a heartfelt moment he wished some type of music was playing to set the mood. Too late now. But next time…

And there would be a next time. He was going to make sure of it. Like he told her, this was *their* place. When he'd made the arrangements on Monday, it had been with her and only her in mind. He hadn't wanted any other woman in that bed with him.

He flinched at the thought, like he always did when his mind would begin thinking of more than sex between them. During those times, he would do whatever was needed to get his thoughts back in check. The only reason he and Rachel were drawn to each other was their intense sexual chemistry. And they were well aware that the attraction could never go beyond what they were sharing now. Neither of them had plans of ever falling in love.

He moved back toward the bed and she shifted on her haunches and met him, reaching out and taking hold of his throbbing erection. She tilted her head back and stared into his eyes for a long moment. Something was passing between them, and he felt it in the hands holding him as well as in the eyes locked with his.

"Tomorrow will we be able to pretend tonight didn't happen?"

Her question broke the silence. "Yes, it's going to be hard but we'll manage it."

She leaned up and licked the side of his face. "You think so?"

"Hell, I hope so, but I'll be the first to admit, every time I see you on the set, I want to tear your clothes off."

He heard her snort at that. "You would have a hard time convincing me of that with that love scene you did today."

He lifted a brow. Love scenes were staged and she was well aware of that. Surely she didn't think any part of them meant anything to him. He was simply following the script. Did he hear a bit of jealousy in her voice?

"Then I need to do whatever it takes to erase that scene from your mind," he said, and for emphasis he reached out and pulled her closer toward him.

He felt the shiver that passed through her and, in response, a slew of emotions flowed through him, nearly taking his breath away. A need for her filled him to capacity, and for a moment he could imagine her with him even when he was in his eighties.

At the thought, he went momentarily still. Where had that come from? He knew there was no way he could consider anything with her beyond this affair.

He reminded himself of that again as he captured her mouth with his and lowered her body to the bed.

There was something about being pressed into the mattress by the man you wanted. A man who was holding her gaze as he entered her slowly, as if he was savoring the journey.

The last time they'd made love he had taken her hard and fast, and now the slowness was driving her mad. She could only ask, "Why?"

He knew what she was asking and said throatily, "There's no rush. We have plenty of time and I want to take things slow, draw it out and make you scream. A lot of times."

She could feel the hardness of him grow inside of her and knew he intended to make some point. Being the skilled lover he was, he'd succeed in making all his wishes come true.

Chapter 12

"Quiet on the set!

"Take one!

"Action!"

Rachel fought back the rush of jealousy as she watched yet another love scene being shot between Dr. Tyrell Perry and Dr. Sonja Duncan. Did Ethan have to appear to be enjoying it so much?

Usually she stayed in the trailer working with the actors, but today she decided to venture out and would be the first to admit a part of her had wanted to see Ethan. More than once he had accused her of hiding out in the trailer, so today she had decided to be seen.

Although, she thought as a smile touched her lips, hiding out in the trailer hadn't stopped him from seeking her out on occasion and making the find worth his while. He had introduced her to quickies. She didn't want to think about the risk they took of someone discovering their secret. So far no one had, and she was thankful for that.

It had been a week since that night when they'd started their secret rendezvous. Most of the time they would meet up at their hideaway haven but on occasion he would come to her place. So far he was still outsmarting the paparazzi.

She smiled, thinking about how Ethan had bought her a disguise—a honey-blond wig and green contacts. And because she was a makeup artist, it hadn't been difficult to add her own camouflage to make herself unrecognizable when they'd made a decision to branch out beyond the bedroom to grab something to eat. They had even risked going to a movie together.

On more than one occasion she had found herself thinking just how a normal relationship with him would be, one where they wouldn't have to sneak around to be together. But she knew such a thing wasn't possible.

"Cut!"

The production crew rushed around trying to get the props changed for another taping, and it was then that Ethan glanced over at her. When he winked and smiled, she couldn't help smiling back. Last night they had spent the night together at *their* place, and he had surprised her by having an easel with art supplies waiting for her when she had arrived. After having made love, he reclined on the bed while she painted him, something he had surprised her by agreeing to do. It would be her own personal painting of him in all his naked splendor to be shared with no one.

She had returned to the trailer when her cell phone went off. Caller ID indicated it was Charlene. "Yes, Cha?"

"I know you don't read the tabloids so I feel I should give you the scoop."

She raised a brow. "About what?"

"Ethan. He's driving the paparazzi crazy by eluding them every chance he gets. They've begun wondering what's going on with him and who the woman he's intent on hiding is."

Rachel felt a knot in her stomach. "Do they have any idea? Did they mention a name?"

"No, but they have vowed to find out, so you might want to cool things with him for a while."

Rachel began nibbling on her bottom lip. Yes, that would be best, but it would be hard to do.

"The media can be relentless when they want to find out something," Charlene added.

Rachel knew that to be true. "Thanks for keeping me in the loop. I appreciate it."

"What are you going to do?"

Rachel drew in a deep breath. She had few options and knew there was only one thing that she could do. Regardless of whether she liked it or whether she was ready for it to happen, their affair had run its course. "I'm going to talk to him."

"And if the two of you meet up somewhere to have

this talk, you might want to be looking over your shoulder. Disguise or no disguise, the two of you will have the media hounds on your heels for sure."

Ethan glanced in his rearview mirror. He was being followed. A deep frown set into his features. He'd been trying to elude the guy now for a full hour without any success.

He was to meet Rachel at *their* place and he couldn't do so as long as this reporter was still on his tail. Even switching cars and donning his disguise hadn't helped. This guy was on to him and seemed intent on letting him know it.

When his cell phone rang, he almost snatched it off his belt and his frown deepened when he saw the caller was Curtis. He had been trying to avoid his agent for a week or so now. "Yes, Curtis?"

"Damn, Ethan, are you trying to mess up a good thing?"

Ethan glanced into his rearview mirror, getting more agitated by the minute. He needed to get rid of this reporter so he could hook up with Rachel at their scheduled time. "What are you talking about?"

"The tabloids. You've become elusive over the past few weeks, annoying the hell out of several tabloid reporters who even claim you've purposely given them the slip."

Ethan rolled his eyes. "And?"

"And they are wondering why and just who you're trying to hide. Someone has connected you to a nameless married woman and has vowed to uncover her identity."

Ethan's hand tightened on the steering wheel. That was not what he wanted to hear. He of all people knew how tabloid reporters could make a pest of themselves more so than usual when they thought they were on to a story.

"I'd like to see them try to uncover anything," he said, almost in a growl, knowing he would do whatever it took to protect Rachel's identity.

"So you're admitting to being involved with a married woman?"

"I'm not admitting to anything, but if I were, it would be my damn business," he responded.

"Not here in Hollywood, Ethan, and not while we're trying to build your career. You were doing a great job wining and dining the ladies, causing others to take notice and earning the title of this town's newest heartthrob. All of that is what we need to continue to build your image the way we want. I know how important that is to you."

Ethan pulled in a deep breath. Yes, it had been important to him at one time, but now...

"And in that same vein, I have a suggestion for a date for you on Saturday night."

Curtis's words pulled Ethan's concentration back into the conversation. "Excuse me?"

"I said that I have a suggestion for a date for you on Saturday."

Ethan frowned. "What are you talking about, Curtis?"

"I'm talking about Faith Pride. I got a call from her agent who suggested it might be a good idea if the two of you attended the event together."

"I know nothing about an event next Saturday night."

"Sure you do," Curtis insisted. "I sent you the invitation with a mailing confirmation so I know you got it."

He might have gotten it but, like the rest of his mail, he hadn't opened it. His time and the majority of his attention had been given to his sexy pixie, with no regrets. He looked back in his rearview mirror. The man was still there. Damn.

"I'm not going anywhere Saturday night, Curtis."

"What? You can't be serious, Ethan. You have to go. You're hot news and expected to be there. If I didn't know better I'd think you didn't give a damn about your career anymore. I assume you still want one, right?"

"Of course I do!"

"Good, but it sounds like you have a distraction and that isn't good. Get rid of her."

"Come again?"

"I said get rid of her, Ethan. I don't know who she is and frankly I don't care. She's interfering with your life in a negative way. Your actions in keeping her a secret mean she isn't someone you want to be seen with." Curtis paused a moment then said, "Oh, hell, please tell me the person is a she and not a he."

Ethan fought the urge to tell his agent just where he could go. Instead he said, "Bye, Curtis."

"Hey, you didn't answer me."

"And I don't intend to. If you don't know the answer to that then it's time I start looking for another agent."

"Wait, Ethan, I think we—"

Angrily Ethan clicked off the phone. He then glanced back in his rearview mirror and saw the bastard was still on his tail. Deciding he'd had enough, he figured it was time to seriously lose this guy. Increasing his speed, he darted in and out of traffic before making a quick exit off the interstate, only to make a quick right and then a quick left into the parking lot of a car wash.

He smiled, thinking it was his lucky day since there weren't many cars around and immediately drove around the side of the bay. A glance in his rearview mirror showed his stalker speeding by. Backing up, Ethan quickly pulled out and headed back toward the interstate, satisfied for the time being that he'd lost his tail.

Rachel continued to pace the bedroom floor. Ethan had called to say he was on his way but would be late due to "unforeseen circumstances." He hadn't elaborated.

She paused by the bed and drew in a deep breath, remembering her conversation with Charlene. Rachel's common sense was basically telling her that continuing to take risks at this point would be acting irresponsibly. She was an intelligent woman and Ethan was an intelligent man. They had enjoyed each other's companionship but both fully understood that they could not have a future together of any kind. And that was where their similarities ended. Their connection over the past three weeks had only been physical. He didn't love her and she didn't love him.

Then why was the thought of not being with him, not sharing stolen moments any longer, causing her heart to ache?

She began moving again, pacing the floor. He would know something was bothering her the moment he saw her. For one thing, she still had her clothes on, and usually if she was the first to arrive, she would be naked in the bed waiting on him.

She turned when she heard the sound of footsteps and felt the fluttering in her chest when the door slowly opened. She couldn't deny the excitement and joy she felt when her gaze met his blue-gray eyes. It was the same moment of elation she felt whenever she saw him.

He closed the door and leaned against it, holding her gaze for a moment, and then he began slowly unbuttoning his shirt. She knew she should stop him, tell him what she'd heard and that they needed to talk about it.

But she couldn't now.

Her hands automatically went to her skirt and undid the zipper, then slowly shimmied out of it before pulling her blouse over her head. She then kicked off her sandals and by the time they met next to the bed they were both completely naked.

As they tumbled together on the bed, one thought ran through her mind. *So much for talking.*

Chapter 13

An hour or so later, a very satiated Ethan was stretched out in the bed with Rachel in his arms and their legs still entwined. Mentally he was ordering his heart rate to slow down, but it wasn't listening. And his brain cells, which had gotten scrambled after a couple of back-to-back orgasms, were still a jumbled mess. But he didn't mind. In fact, he couldn't imagine it any other way. He was precisely where he wanted to be and was with the one person he wanted to share his time.

He raised her hand to his lips to kiss it and in response she snuggled even closer to him. Her body felt warm all over, and he liked the feel of spooning her backside, cradling her hips.

"So tell me," he leaned down and whispered close

to her ear. "Why were you still wearing clothes when I got here?"

He noticed the exact moment her body stiffened and he tightened his arms around her. Only a man who had been a lover to this woman could detect at that moment she was bothered by something. He shifted his weight, turned her in his arms to face him and his eyes met hers. "What's wrong, Rachel?"

For a moment he wasn't sure she would answer him, and then in a soft voice she said, "My friend Charlene called today."

He was sure there was more. "And?"

"You were in the tabloids. It seems reporters are trying to figure out who's your flavor of the month."

"They wouldn't have to try and figure it out since I'd be glad to tell them, if you would let me."

She stared at him through long lashes, surprise showing in her eyes, and he understood why. This was the first time he'd ever suggested they take their affair public. The only reason he'd never done so was because he knew her feelings on the matter.

"Ethan," she breathed out in a regretful tone. "I can't."

In other words, you won't, he thought and fought back the frustration he felt. He thought about the party and knew he didn't want to take any other woman but her. He pulled in a deep breath, wondering at what point he had decided he wanted more than a fling with her. When had sneaking around with Rachel become something he did only because that was the way she wanted it?

"Okay, you can't," he said, trying to keep the sting from his voice. "What does a tabloid reporter have to do with you having your clothes on when I got here?"

She turned her head to look at the painting of him that she had done and hung on the wall. It was a good thing they were the only ones with keys to this room in the building. He would hate for anyone to ever walk in and see that painting of him. She called it art; he thought of it as borderline X-rated. The only thing keeping him from being completely nude was the very thin piece of cloth that covered a certain part of his body at the juncture of his legs.

"Rachel, you're thinking too much again."

She returned her gaze to his. "Tabloid reporters are trying to figure out who you're spending your time with. You and I know if they keep snooping then it's only a matter of time before they find out, and I can't let that happen, Ethan. I can't risk being placed in the spotlight ever again. And then there's my career I have to think about. I've worked too hard building myself as a professional in the industry to risk losing everything."

He pulled in a deep breath. Those damn reporters had definitely done a job on her when she was a kid for her to have this intense fear. He could just imagine the hell she went through. He pulled her tighter to him, trying to imagine life without her. He would still see her on the set but he had begun thinking of these interludes with her as their time. He looked forward to them. In a way, he needed them. They had stopped being just sexual escapades a while ago. There were those times like these where he would hold her in his arms and savor what they shared, both the physical and the emotional.

"You won't lose anything, Rachel. I told you our secret is safe. No one knows about us or this place."

"For now, but how long will it be before they—"

"Once they see I'm no longer worth their time and effort, they will leave me alone," he interrupted her. "Hmm, as much as I don't want to attend that function Saturday night, maybe I should."

Rachel lifted a brow. "What function?"

"Some charity function Curtis wants me to attend with a date to calm the waters with the tabloids. Maybe if they see I'm a boring person who's gotten so absorbed in my career and nothing more, they will move on to someone else."

He could tell by the look in her eyes that she was confused. "But I thought you wanted to court the media, build your career that way as a playboy."

He studied her features. *I thought so, too,* he said to himself. And instead of trying to determine why he'd had a change of heart, he said, "There are other ways."

He pulled her closer into his arms. "Come on, we've talked enough. Let's get some sleep."

She pulled back. "Sleep?"

He smiled. "Yes, but if you prefer that we didn't…" He leaned over and kissed her in a way that had her body quivering. And when she responded by returning the kiss he proceeded to deepen it.

This was what he wanted and what he needed. Tabloids or no tabloids he intended to keep her by his side, even if they had to continue to sneak around to do it.

Rachel wrapped the sheet around her as she sank into the chair across from the bed. She needed to think and she couldn't do so wrapped in Ethan's arms. She had to have distance.

She closed her eyes and could clearly recall how it felt to be accosted by a crowd of reporters shoving mikes in your face, pulling on your hair to get your attention and all but screaming questions at you. She would try hiding behind her aunt and uncle, and later behind Sofia, but they would get relentless, their questions more demanding, the hordes of reporters even bigger. Then there was the period where she'd had nightmares about them and how they would all enjoy making her life unbearable.

And it had kept up that way until after she'd finished high school and then decided to travel abroad for a while. When she returned home, all the attention had shifted to other heiresses and up-and-coming starlets and actors. They forgot about her, practically left her alone, except for those times when the Wellesley family appeared together at a social function.

Over the years she had worked so hard to avoid that, as well as strived to be taken seriously in the industry as a makeup artist and wardrobe designer. To land a job on one of the most popular television shows was definitely a feather in her cap, one she refused to lose.

But she didn't want to lose Ethan either. She glanced at him, asleep in the bed. She enjoyed these times with him when she could be herself. Although they made love, they spent time talking as well. He had become her lover but he was still her friend, a very good friend. And it was a friendship that she cherished.

"Rachel?"

She heard the sound of her name and glanced toward the bed again. Ethan had awoken and had stretched his hand out to her. Without a moment's hesitation, she eased from the chair, dropped the sheet and went to him.

He gathered her into his arms and whispered, "You're thinking again and that's not a good thing."

She pulled back and looked up at him and smiled. "It's not?"

"No."

"Well, then, can you come up with a better pastime?"

He rubbed his nose against her neck. "Um, I think I can," he said throatily before capturing her mouth.

He released her mouth and eased her down on the

bed. "Yes," she managed hoarsely, as her body began shivering in a need only he could satisfy, "I believe you can."

A few days later Rachel looked down into the face of the actress reclining in her makeup chair and smiled before handing the woman the mirror. "There you go. Your makeup looks good on you, as always."

Livia studied her features in the mirror and smiled. "And, as always, you did a wonderful job, Rachel. You certainly know your stuff."

Rachel thanked her. Livia Blake was always giving her compliments about her work. Unlike Tae'Shawna Miller. The woman was still living in a fantasy world, still weaving the story of a secret affair with Ethan. Rachel figured she was the only one the woman had probably shared her lie with, probably because she figured Rachel was the only person gullible enough to believe her.

"You're one of the few people I'm going to miss when I leave the show," Livia said, easing up in her chair and handing the mirror back to Rachel.

Rachel knew she was going to miss Livia as well. Over the past weeks, she'd discovered her earlier assumptions about the woman had been all false, especially when she'd taken time to compare her to Tae'Shawna. Both were beautiful women who turned men's heads without much effort. But their attitudes and the way they treated people were totally different. Livia wasn't shallow or self-absorbed at all. Tae'Shawna took all those honors.

"You know how directors are. They may decide to rewrite the script and keep you on."

Livia shook her head sadly. "I doubt that will happen, although it would be wonderful. I'm thirty and nearing the end of my modeling career and although it's been a good one, it's time I moved on, although I haven't figured out to where just yet. *Paging the Doctor* has been a stepping-stone in the right direction. I've met some good people on the set, and—" she threw her head back and chuckled "—a few not so good ones."

Rachel smiled. Livia didn't have to tell her who the "not so good ones" were. Everyone had figured out by now there were several women on the set who were jealous of Livia's beauty, with Tae'Shawna heading the list.

"Well, I wish you the best," Rachel said sincerely.

"And I wish you the best, as well." Livia paused and then said, "Can I offer you some advice, though?"

Rachel raised a brow. "Advice about what?"

"Not what, but who. Ethan Chambers."

With effort, Rachel kept her features expressionless as she continued to pack away her cosmetics. "Ethan?" she asked, fighting to keep her voice steady. "And what kind of advice do you want to offer me about him?"

Livia paused, as if trying to choose her words carefully, and then she said, "I know the two of you are fiercely attracted to each other and…"

When Rachel began shaking her head, trying to deny it, Livia waved her off. "Hey, I felt the vibes between the two of you, even during his hot and heavy love scenes with me."

"But I—"

"Want to deny it," Livia said, smiling. "I don't know why you would want to when you're both beautiful people. Look, I'm sorry if mentioning it got you all flustered. That wasn't my intent. I just don't know why the two of you are keeping it a secret."

Rachel dropped down in the nearest chair, totally outdone. She and Ethan had worked so hard not to give anything away on the set, yet Livia had picked up on it. She met Livia's curious gaze. "Do you think others noticed?"

Livia shrugged. "Probably not. I'm just good at reading people and picking up vibes. I doubt Tae'Shawna noticed, since she's under the illusion he's all into her, and Paige isn't any better. Those are the only two still hanging on, hoping he'll give them some attention. I think the other women on the set have decided he's truly not interested."

Rachel didn't say anything for a moment, and then asked, "What did we do to give ourselves away?"

Livia chuckled. "The way the two of you look at each other when you think no one else is noticing, and I'm sure no one else is noticing but me, only because I have a tendency to notice everything. But I still don't understand why the two of you are keeping it a secret."

Rachel nibbled at her bottom lip. "It's complicated. I prefer not being in the limelight and he's a person who can't help but be there, dead center."

"Well, I hope things work out for the two of you because I think you're a good match, and you and Ethan truly deserve each other. Since I've gotten to know the both of you, I can easily see you're good people."

Livia glanced down at her watch. "It's time for me to get ready for my next scene. I'm not sure how they plan to write in my exit from the show since I'm supposedly Dr. Perry's love interest with emotional baggage. I think I'm supposed to pack up and leave when things between us get hot and heavy because I haven't gotten over my husband's death."

Rachel nodded. It was either that or killing Dr. Duncan off, but she couldn't see them doing that. Still, on the set, you never knew how things would go.

"Ethan, can I see you for a moment?"

Ethan kept the annoyance out of his face as he turned around. "Yes, Tae'Shawna, what is it?"

She smiled up at him. "I have tickets to the premier of *Saturday's Hussle*. Would you like to go with me tonight?"

Ethan knew just where he planned to be tonight, and Rachel's arms were far better than any movie premier. Even if he and Rachel hadn't made plans to meet up later, Tae'Shawna would be the last woman he'd go out with. "Thanks, but I have plans already."

"Oh. Maybe next time."

He doubted it. In fact, he knew for certain there wouldn't be a first time or a next time. "I'll see you later," he said, turning to leave.

"Umm, you don't know how I wish on that one, Ethan."

He kept walking, refusing to turn back around and respond to her flirty comment. His workday had ended, and for him, the fun was about to begin with the woman he wanted.

Chapter 14

Rachel glanced over at Charlene as they got out of the car. They were at a karaoke bar for a girls' night out. It was Saturday night and Ethan had decided to go to the charity event solo, against his agent's wishes. He'd insisted he would not take a date.

"Are you ready to have some fun?" she asked her friend. Rachel knew she needed to cheer Charlene up since her mother had hit again, calling her and telling her younger daughter all the reasons why she couldn't get a man.

"Yes, although you should have let me spend the weekend alone getting wasted."

Rachel laughed. "Neither one of us can handle too

much booze and we both know it. Come on, let's enjoy ourselves."

A few hours later they were doing just that. Rachel was trying to talk Charlene into competing in the singing contest to win the five-hundred-dollar prize. Everyone knew what a beautiful voice she had.

"You really think I should?" Charlene asked.

Rachel smiled. Charlene had a dynamite voice but she'd always had this thing about singing in public. She much preferred staying behind the scenes, working as a voice coach at one of the local schools. "Hey, so far I haven't been impressed by the others I've heard. The sound of your voice has spoiled me. Personally, I think you have a good shot at winning. Just think of what you could do with the money." And Rachel could see from her best friend's expression that she was thinking the same thing.

"I don't know, Rachel."

"Well, I do, so just think about it. You have time to make up your mind. We're going to be here for a while."

And she meant it. She wasn't ready to go home to sit around or go to bed wondering if Ethan was having a good time at that event without her. No doubt there would be plenty of women there throwing themselves at him. She pulled in a deep breath. By mutual agreement, they were in an exclusive relationship. She knew she hadn't dated anyone else since they'd begun sleeping together and he'd said he hadn't either.

"Okay, I'm going to do it!"

Charlene's exclamation interrupted Rachel's thoughts and she smiled over at her friend. "Good. I have a feeling that you won't regret it."

The hounds were on Ethan the minute he got out of his car.

"Chambers? Where have you been hiding?" a reporter asked as a mike was shoved in Ethan's face and cameras went off from all directions.

Stepping into his role, he smiled for the cameras. "I haven't been hiding."

That began a series of other questions and he answered every last one of them with the intent of diffusing their curiosity and getting them interested in his role in *Paging the Doctor* instead. After a while it worked, although there were still a couple of reporters who seemed determined to dig into his personal life. Years of being one of the heirs to the Chambers Winery had taught him how to handle that kind.

"No date, Ethan?" one of the two resilient reporters asked.

"No, no date. Is there anything wrong with a man coming alone?"

"Not when he doesn't have to," was the other resilient reporter's quick comeback.

Ethan smiled. "I call it freedom of choice."

He answered a few more questions before bidding the reporters good-night. He knew he would be tailed when he left the event, but he figured eventually they would reach the conclusion he was no longer newsworthy and go find someone else to harass.

"I can't believe I won!"

Rachel smiled brightly over at Charlene who was holding a bottle of champagne in one hand and a check for five hundred dollars in the other. "I told you that you would. I keep telling you that you have a beautiful voice. Maybe one day you'll finally believe me." Charlene had done a beautiful rendition of "Bridge Over Troubled Water" and brought everyone out of their seats. "You sounded like a young Aretha."

Charlene waved off her words. "You're my best friend, so of course you'd think so, and you know how much I love me some Aretha."

Yes, Rachel did know, but no matter what Charlene thought, she was dead serious.

"Excuse me, ladies."

Both Rachel and Charlene glanced at the man standing by their table. "Yes?" Charlene asked.

"I hate interrupting, but I wanted to congratulate you, Ms. Quinn. You did an outstanding job. And I want to introduce myself. I'm Jason Burke, a talent scout," he said handing Charlene his card. "Please call me. I would like to discuss a few things with you. The company I represent would love to bring you on board."

Rachel could tell from the look on Charlene's face that she wasn't taking the man seriously. Playing along with him, Charlene slid his card into her pocket and said, "Sure, I'd love to contact you. Will next week be soon enough?"

The man smiled brightly. "Yes, and I'll look forward to that call." He then walked away and out of the club.

Charlene rolled her eyes. "Does he really think I'm going to call him?"

Rachel took a sip of her drink. "You said that you would."

"That was to get rid of him. Please. I can sing but not that good. And he's probably not who he's claiming to be."

"Let me see his business card." Rachel waited while Charlene dug it out of the pocket of her jeans.

Rachel studied the card. "I think you should call Sofia and let her check him out to see if he's legit. If he is, I would follow up with him if I were you."

Charlene waved off her words. "Whatever. Hey, let's forget about Jason Burke and have a good time. We need to get on the dance floor and celebrate my win."

Rachel laughed as she followed Charlene onto the floor to shake their booties for a while.

It was past three in the morning by the time Rachel had showered and slid between the sheets. She was about to turn off the lamp when her cell phone rang. Thinking it was Charlene still on a high from that night's win, she answered the phone saying, "Hey, haven't you gotten enough already?"

"Of you? Never."

Her body immediately began throbbing at the sound

of the deep, husky voice. Her eyes clouded over in desire just from hearing it. "Hey, lover boy, haven't you heard it's not nice to call a girl after midnight?"

His soft chuckle came through the phone and touched her in places she'd rather leave untouched. But since he was going there, she might as well let him finish. "I prefer being there in person but some ass is parked outside the complex, waiting for me to leave. So I guess I'll stay in and engage in some sex talk with you."

She chuckled. "Sounds like a winner to me. Speaking of wins, Charlene won a singing contest at the club tonight. A whopping five hundred dollars and a bottle of champagne. And a talent scout approached her afterwards."

"I'm happy for her."

Although Ethan and Charlene had never officially met, they knew a lot about each other thanks to Rachel. "I'll tell her you are." There was a pause, and then she asked, "And how was your night?"

"Boring."

"Did you change your mind about taking a date with you?"

"No."

Rachel tried not to feel giddy at that one single word but couldn't help it. She had convinced herself that she could handle it if he'd decided to take a date. After all, they were nothing more to each other than occasional bed partners. She drew in a deep breath, not wanting to think about it or how depressed she'd get when she did.

"So what are you wearing?"

His question made her smile. "What makes you think I'm wearing anything?"

He chuckled. "You only sleep naked when you're with me."

"Says who?"

"Says me. The man who has made love to you a lot of times."

"Hmm, how many?" she asked in what she hoped was a sexy, low tone. And he was right. He had made love to her a lot of times.

"Was I supposed to be counting?"

"I was."

He laughed. "Okay, then how many?"

"Tally up your own numbers, Chambers."

"If I were there, I would tickle it out of you."

"If you were here, Ethan, I'd make sure you put your hands to more productive use."

When Rachel hung up the phone an hour later she drew in a deep breath. Ethan's smooth, hot talk had almost made her come several times, it definitely had made her consider leaving her house and meeting him somewhere. But luckily her common sense held tight. They had agreed to throw the paparazzi off their scent by not meeting at their place anytime during the coming week. That meant when they did get back together for some bed time, they would have a whole lot of making up to do.

Ethan left his home on Sunday morning to go to the diner for some coffee and a roll. When he walked out with his purchase, he noticed one of the reporters from last night was waiting on him, braced against Ethan's car. The man was Joe Connors and he was known to be as tenacious as they came.

Since he was wearing the same clothes as he'd worn yesterday when he'd followed him, Joe had apparently slept in his car. And because Ethan considered himself a good guy, while buying breakfast for himself he'd also grabbed something for Joe.

"Looks like you could use this as much as I can," Ethan said, handing the man the extra breakfast sack he had in his hand. "All the creamers, sugars and artificial sweeteners you'll ever need are in that bag," he added.

The man accepted the offering. He then took a sip of the coffee, drinking it black. "Good stuff. Thanks."

"You're welcome." Ethan took a sip of his own coffee and asked, "Now, why don't you be a nice guy and leave me alone."

Joe chuckled as he shook his head. "No can do. I have to make a living."

"Don't we all?" was Ethan's dry response.

The man eyed him curiously. "Since you're in a giving mood, Chambers, how about an interview?"

Ethan shook his head. "I gave you an interview last night. You asked your questions and I answered them."

"Yes, but you refused to talk about your love life."

Ethan smiled. "What makes you think I have a love life?"

The man shrugged. "I just figured you did. This time

last year you were dating anything in a skirt, and now for the past month you've been cooling your heels, so to speak, which can only mean you've been caught."

"Caught?"

"Yes. Some woman's got your heart. Is she married?"

Ethan threw his head back and laughed. "What is this obsession that I'm involved with a married woman?"

"What other reason would make you go to great pains to hide her?"

Ethan fought back the temptation to respond by saying he wasn't trying to hide Rachel. He would be perfectly happy if they made their affair public but...

"Um, look's like you started to say something and then changed your mind. Did I get close to the truth or something?"

"No."

"You sure?"

"Positive."

Joe looked at him for the longest time. "Then what was that funny look about?"

"Nothing. Eat your food, Joe. It's getting cold."

After pulling a warm croissant from the bag, Joe tilted his head and looked at Ethan. He grinned and said, "Hey man, you're not such a bad guy."

Chapter 15

"Have a nice evening, Rachel."

Rachel smiled over at one of her assistants. "You do the same, Loraine."

"And don't hang around here too late. They start killing the lights around seven," Loraine advised.

"Thanks for letting me know that."

There were only a few more weeks of filming left before the final shoot of the season. A wrap party was already being planned and Frasier was going all out to make it a monumental affair.

As she thought about the season ending, Rachel was happy that Livia's character was not killed off. It left the door open for a possible return next season. Just as she had predicted, Dr. Duncan was not emotionally ready for a hot and heavy love affair with Dr. Perry so soon after her husband's death. The season would end with her asking to be transferred to another hospital in Florida. That meant Dr. Perry would be free to pursue another love interest next season.

Livia would be joining her and Charlene for dinner over the weekend. Ever since Livia had mentioned that she was aware of her affair with Ethan, the two of them had become friends. Rachel appreciated Livia not gossiping about her and Ethan; apparently somebody in Hollywood could keep a secret.

Rachel's cell phone went off and she pulled it out of the pocket of her smock. "Yes?"

"Whooo, Rachel, you'll never guess what happened to me!"

Rachel couldn't help but hear the excitement in Charlene's voice. "And what has happened to you?"

"That guy Jason Burke is legit. Sofia checked him out. He works in A&R for the big music company that distributes Playascape."

Rachel lifted a brow. Playascape was a well-known recording company. One of the biggies. "Are you sure?"

"Sofia verified everything."

Then that settled it. Sofia knew just about everyone in the music, movie and television industry through Limelight Entertainment.

"And guess what?"

"What?"

"They want me to come in and meet with them."

Rachel couldn't help but be ecstatic as well. "Wow, Cha, that's fantastic."

"I think so, too, and Sofia suggested I send them a copy of that demo tape I did a while back."

"That's a smart move."

"Sofia's managing everything for me."

Rachel's smile widened. She knew her sister's abilities when it came to working deals. "Then you're in good hands."

Rachel heard a sound and turned around. Her breath caught in her throat when she saw Ethan. He had entered the trailer and was leaning against the closed door. Their eyes met and she watched as he reached behind him and locked it. The click sounded loud.

"Cha, that's good news but I need to call you back later."

"You okay?"

Evidently Charlene had heard the change in her voice. "Yes, I'm fine. I'll call you when I get home." She then clicked off the phone.

"Ethan, what are you doing here? I thought you'd left hours ago."

He crossed his arms over his chest. Instead of answering her, he had a question of his own. "And why are you still here?"

"I had some paperwork to do."

He checked his watch. "It's late."

"I know but I'm fine. The security guard patrolling the studio lot is still here."

He was still leaning against the door, but now

his hands were tucked into the pockets of his jeans. Although they saw each other every day on the set, they hadn't been together intimately for over a week thanks to that tabloid reporter dogging Ethan's heels. But they did talk on the phone every night and had made plans to try and sneak away to Tijuana this weekend.

"Go ahead and finish what you have to do. I'll wait and walk you out to your car."

She swallowed the lump in her throat. "That's not necessary."

"I think it is."

Instead of arguing with him she slid behind her small desk and began going over the paperwork she needed to give John in the morning. Out of the corner of her eye she saw Ethan had moved away from the door to straddle one of the chairs.

The air-conditioning system was working but she was beginning to feel hot. She was also feeling his eyes on her, singeing her flesh. In the quiet, she couldn't help but be aware of him. He'd been in the trailer with her lots of times while she'd applied his makeup, and because of where they were, things had always been professional between them. But she'd always been tempted with him reclining in one of her chairs and her over him and breathing in his scent.

Deciding the trailer was too quiet, she opted to share Charlene's good news with him. "Isn't that wonderful?"

"Yeah, I think it's great," he replied. "I hear they have a good outfit over there."

Rachel continued working, going through John's requests for the season finale. Out of the corner of her eye, she saw that Ethan had moved again. This time he'd gone over to the watercooler to get something to drink. She turned to look at him at the exact time he tilted the cup up to his lips to take a swallow.

The way his throat moved as water trickled down it did something to her. And when he licked his lips as if the drink had been one of the most refreshing things to go into his mouth, she actually began envying the water.

"How much longer before you're done?"

She blinked and realized he had spoken to her. In that case, he'd probably caught her staring. She drew in a deep breath as she looked down at the papers. "Not long. If you need to leave then I—"

"No, I don't need to leave. But I do need you."

Now *that* she heard. And upon doing so, she couldn't smother the heated sensations taking root in the pit of her stomach or the hot tingle between her legs. This was where she worked, her business sanctuary. Actors came and went and usually she was too busy, too involved to connect the insides of this trailer to any one particular person. But for some reason, she had a feeling that was about to change.

Deciding not to respond to what he'd said, she turned her attention back to the papers in front of her. Ten minutes later, she was signing off on the last sheet. She opened the top drawer to slide them inside.

"Finished now?"

She glanced over at him and met his gaze. He had gone back to straddling one of the chairs. "Yes."

"Good." He stood. "Come here, Rachel."

She continued to hold his gaze, felt the heat zinging between the two of them. She didn't have to ask what he wanted; the look on his face told her what he needed. It was there in his expression, in the chiseled and handsome features. Not to mention those beautiful eyes staring back at her.

Instead of putting up any fuss, not that she would have, she crossed the room without a word and walked straight into his arms. He pulled her to him and she felt it all. His heat, the pounding of his heart against her chest and the engorged erection pressing at the juncture of her thighs.

"It's been hell these seven days without you," he whispered against her lips.

"Actually, it's been eight but who's counting?" she said as her arms automatically went around his waist and she rested her head against his chest. She had to fight hard to keep from being overwhelmed by him. When she felt his erection throb against her thigh, she pulled back and glanced up at him.

"We'll be together Saturday," she reminded him.

He smiled down at her but she still saw the tension in his features. "I can't wait. I need you now."

As he spoke, he backed her against the wall. Already his hands at her waist were lifting her up. Instead of wearing jeans today she had decided to wear a skirt. *How convenient for him,* she thought.

And for her.

Her legs automatically wrapped around him and his hands were busy under her skirt, pushing her panties aside before unzipping his pants and freeing himself. By mutual consent, he had stopped using condoms when she'd told him she was on the pill.

His finger slid inside her as if to test her readiness, and the feel of his touch had her moaning.

"Shh," he whispered in her ear. "There's no need to bring the guard in here to check out things."

No, there was no reason, which meant she couldn't let go and scream. How was she going to stop it? He always made her scream.

His finger inside her was driving her to the brink. He'd said he needed her and he was taking his time to make sure that she also needed him. She should tell him doing so wasn't necessary. She did need him. She did need this.

"Baby, you're hot and your scent is driving me insane," he whispered before taking her mouth in a kiss that told her this was just the beginning.

He covered her lips, captured her mouth in a combination of hunger and tenderness that zapped her senses. And when his tongue began doing its thing, exploring her mouth as if it were conquering unfamiliar territory, she went weak in the knees. But he held her, making sure she didn't go anywhere. She had detected his hunger the minute he'd entered the trailer, and now she was experiencing it firsthand.

Her body was responding to him as it always did

and as it always would. Whenever it came to this kind of mutual satisfaction, they were always in accord. A deep, throbbing ache within her intensified and, of its own will, the lower part of her body rocked against his. She clung to him as his mouth clung to hers, plundering it, stirring sensations all the way down to the soles of her feet.

For one fleeting moment she felt the silky head of his erection probe her womanly core, then he entered her in one smooth stroke. She wrapped her legs around him to take him in fully.

She moaned into his mouth and gripped tightly to his shoulders, surrendering to the feel of him being embedded within her, stretching her wide. He deepened the kiss and at the same time he began to move, thrusting back and forth inside of her, feeding her hunger while making her skin tingle all over. Her breasts felt heavy, full and sensitive to the chest rubbing against them.

He was deep inside her and with each thrust he was going deeper still. As he rocked his hips against her, he used his hands to cushion her back from the wall.

He pulled his mouth away and whispered against her lips, "Come for me, baby. I need to feel you come."

As if his words were a command for her body to obey, she felt herself begin to shatter into a million pieces. She clenched her teeth to hold back her scream, and when his mouth came down on hers she gave in and felt every part of her body explode in a climax so intense she trembled all over.

"That's it, baby. Now I'm yours," he uttered huskily

right before his body ignited in an explosion as well. She felt the hot, thick essence of him shoot all the way inside of her in the most primitive way, and she called out his name.

He responded in kind, and the sound of her name on his lips sent everything within her throbbing for more. She only knew this kind of pleasure with him. She only wanted this kind of pleasure from him.

Sensation spiraled inside of her and she knew at that moment that Ethan Chambers had captured her heart.

Chapter 16

"Ethan, wait. I need to see you for a moment."

Ethan looked over his shoulder and turned around. "I was on my way out, Paige. What's up?"

Joe Connors had finally stopped being his shadow, but that didn't mean he and Rachel could let their guard down. They'd been careful since that amazing night in the trailer, not hooking up until last weekend in Tijuana. Their Mexican rendezvous had been special, and they'd made up for the time they'd lost. Now they would be spending the night at *their* place and Ethan couldn't wait. He didn't need Paige Stiles delaying him.

"Evidently you're up, big boy," she said in that flirty voice that annoyed the hell out of him. "I need a date to the wrap party."

He chuckled softly. "And?"

"And you're going to take me."

He was surprised by her bold statement. He had finally gotten Tae'Shawna out of his hair by his persistence in letting her know he wasn't interested. Paige, on the other hand, was not getting the message. He'd just have to be more explicit. "I'm not taking you anywhere."

"Yes, you are. At least, you will if you want me to keep your secret."

He felt the hair stand up on the back of his neck. "And just what secret is that?"

"You banging Rachel Wellesley. She never fooled me. I figured she had the hots for you just as bad as the next woman, and I was wondering how long it would take for you to be lured by her bait." The woman then chuckled. "Seriously, Ethan, are you *that* hard up? You couldn't do better than Rachel? If I was picking someone that you'd want to mess around with, it wouldn't be her. And don't deny the two of you are involved because I can prove it."

He drew in a deep breath, not sure if she could prove it but truly not caring. "No, I seriously don't think I can do better than Rachel. Now if you will excuse me, I—"

"I mean it, Ethan. You make plans to get something going with me or else."

"Or else what?"

She smiled sweetly. "Or else everyone, especially Frasier and John, will know that Rachel isn't the sweetie pie they think she is."

Now that pushed his anger to the top. "I don't know what game you're playing, Paige, but keep Rachel out of this."

"Sure, I'll keep her out of this, but only if you give me what I want. My name connected to yours will open doors. I not only want those doors opened, I want to walk through them."

"It won't happen."

She wiped the smile from her face. "Then I suggest that you make sure it does."

She walked away.

On the drive home, Ethan tried to figure out the best way to handle Paige. Reasoning with her was out of the question since the woman was vindictive and obviously intent on hurting Rachel. He had detected her dislike and jealousy from the first.

The one thing he'd learned growing up as a Chambers was to not let anyone bully, or in this case blackmail, you into doing something you did not want to do. He had no intention of taking Paige or any other woman to the wrap party. The only woman he would take was the woman he wanted and would always want. Rachel.

He thought about telling Rachel about Paige's threats, but he could just imagine what her reaction would be. He wanted to save her from that worry. And he wanted to save himself from seeing it. No, he would simply ignore Paige as he had Tae'Shawna and hopefully she would forget about her foolish threat.

He had no problems with his and Rachel's relationship going public and he'd pushed for that several times with

Rachel—only to meet a brick wall. For some reason she thought news of their involvement would diminish the professional career she had created, and then there was her intense desire not to be in the spotlight.

There was no one who could say his and Rachel's relationship on the set had been anything other than professional. And as far as her being in the spotlight, he thought she didn't give herself enough credit for handling things. He knew the media could sometimes be relentless, but because of their families, he and Rachel had been born into the spotlight anyway and the key was not avoiding it but dealing with it.

As he continued on the drive home, he finally admitted something else. Something he'd known for a while but just hadn't acknowledged. He had fallen in love with Rachel. And because he loved her, he didn't want to sneak around to be with her. He wanted everyone to know the woman he loved and adored, the woman who could make him smile just by being close to him. The woman he wanted to bring home to meet his family.

The woman he wanted to marry.

He wanted Rachel, and only Rachel, to become Mrs. Ethan Chambers. He wanted her to be the mother of his children. To walk by his side for always.

He gripped the steering wheel, knowing those thoughts were true. Every single one of them. But they were thoughts he could not share with Rachel. She didn't love him, and she didn't want to share a future with him.

* * *

Two days later Paige was back in his face again, reiterating her demands.

Ethan gave her his total attention, squaring off and looking her right in the eyes with an adamant expression. "Look, Paige, I told you once before that I'm not taking you to the wrap party and I meant it. My feelings haven't changed."

He saw the anger build in her features. Her jaw clenched and her eyes narrowed. "Then you leave me no choice. Now everyone will know what you and Rachel have been doing behind their backs."

Then she walked off.

Ethan got into his car, pissed but still positive he was handling the nagging woman the only way he could. He decided to forgo the air-conditioning on the ride home, preferring the warm breeze against his face. He imagined the stench of Paige Stiles being blown off him.

As if he'd warded it away, any thought of the encounter dared not enter his mind. Until the next night when his cell phone rang.

How Joe Connors, of all people, had gotten his cell phone number, Ethan didn't know and didn't waste his time asking.

"What do you want, Connors?" he asked instead.

"I like you, Chambers. You're different from most of the stars out there who can be anal, so I'm giving you a heads-up. You and your lady have been exposed. Not by me, but by a tip we received. And there are pictures, nothing sleazy, but pictures that will substantiate this person's claim. They are pretty damn excited over here, and I understand the article, pictures and all, hits tomorrow's paper."

Ethan felt his heart drop to his feet. He drew in a deep breath, knowing he had to get in touch with Rachel. She had volunteered to be a chaperone to Disneyland for a group of kids who attended the school where Charlene worked as a voice coach. She wasn't scheduled to return until late tonight.

When Ethan didn't say anything, Joe Connors continued, "I can't give you details but I can tell you the headline of the article isn't pretty."

Dread turned to anger, and it raced through Ethan. "Thanks for the heads-up."

Ending the call, he tried to reach Rachel. He had to prepare her for whatever the article said and assure her they would handle it, work through it and deal with it.

He only hoped she'd believe him.

Rachel finished taking her shower and was about to settle in for the night when she checked her messages on her cell phone. She lifted a brow. She had several missed calls from Ethan and just as many text messages and they all said the same thing: "Call ASAP."

Wondering at the urgency, she was about to punch in his phone number when there was loud knock at her door. After running downstairs she took a quick look through her peephole and saw Ethan. She quickly opened her door.

"Ethan, what is—"

He suddenly pulled her into his arms and kissed her, kicking the door closed behind him as he continued kissing her and sweeping her off her feet, into his arms.

She always enjoyed being kissed by him and today was no exception. His lips moved hungrily over hers and instinctively she melted against him, loving the feel of being in his arms. She whimpered his name when moments later he pulled his mouth away.

"Rachel, sweetheart, we need to talk."

She saw they were no longer at the door, but he had carried her across the room and had taken a seat on the sofa with her cradled in his arms. She had been so wrapped up in their kiss she hadn't noticed the movement.

It was then that she remembered the missed calls and text messages. "What about?" Her voice sounded wobbly from the impact of his kiss.

He continued to hold her tightly against him and when he didn't answer her, she glanced up into his eyes. She had been with Ethan long enough to know when he was deeply troubled. She pulled herself up. "What is it, Ethan?"

"I need to prepare you for something."

"What?"

"The tabloids know about us, thanks to Paige, and *The Wagging Tongue* is breaking the story tomorrow. Someone I know on the inside called and gave me a heads-up."

Rachel felt as if someone had just doused her with a pail of cold water right in her face. She jumped out of his lap. "What?"

"Yes, baby, I know. This is not how you wanted things, but together we'll deal with it."

She backed away from him. "No, no, this can't be happening..." Shaking her head as if to get her thoughts in order, she asked, "What does Paige have to do with it?"

Ethan rubbed his hand over his face. "Earlier in the week she approached me claiming she knew about us and threatening to go to Frasier and John if I didn't begin dating her. She figured her name connected to mine would take her places. I flatly refused and two days ago, when she approached me again and I refused again, she got mad. I guess this is her way of getting retaliation."

Rachel's head began pounding. "She approached you earlier in the week and you didn't mention it to me?"

He came to his feet and faced her. "I didn't want to upset you and I was hoping she would drop it."

Rachel pulled in a deep breath. "Paige is like a sore that only festers. She's never cared for me, Ethan. Jealousy is deeply embedded in any decision she makes about me. She's always wanted you, and for her to find out you and I have been involved in an affair, there's no way she would have dropped it. You should have told me."

"Maybe I should have, but I didn't want you upset."

"Well, now I am upset. I am livid. I am mad as hell."

He reached out for her. "The truth is out, baby, and we'll deal with it."

She pulled away from him. "It's not that easy, Ethan. It's my privacy and professionalism being threatened."

"And I still say we will deal with it, Rachel. When we're approached we'll tell them the truth."

"No, we won't! We will deny everything. They can't prove anything."

"I'm not sure about that. The person I talked to claims there are pictures."

"Pictures! Oh my God!" She dropped down on the sofa and covered her face with her hands.

Ethan went to her and pulled her into his arms. He'd never seen her this upset. "Rachel, the best thing to do is not to deny anything. We're two consenting adults who—"

"Should not have let things get out of hand. We should not have gotten involved in the first place since we knew what was at risk."

"But we did and we need to own up to it and not let the tabloids or anyone else control our lives or our relationship."

She jerked out of his arms. "No! You make it sound so easy and it's not. Don't you understand what I'll be going through, Ethan? Don't you understand? You like this sort of stuff. It makes you who you are, but it can only destroy me."

"Rachel, we can deal with it. Together."

"No! That's just it. We can't be together. That will just be more fuel for their fire. We have to end things between us now."

"That's not going to happen, Rachel. I won't give you up because of any damn tabloid," he said angrily.

She glared up at him. "You don't have a choice because I'm ending things between us, Ethan. I can't sacrifice a professional career I've worked hard to build or a private life I've tried hard to preserve. Besides, our affair was about nothing but sex anyway."

Her words were like a backhanded slap to Ethan's face and he felt the pain in the depths of his heart. "You don't mean that, Rachel," he said softly.

He refused to believe all the time they'd spent together had been about nothing but sex. Maybe that had been the case the first few times, but there was no way he would believe she didn't care for him the way he cared for her. No way.

"I love you, Rachel. Our times together weren't just about sex for me and I refuse to believe that's the way it was for you. And I won't deny what we shared to anyone. I won't make it into some backstreet, sleazy affair. I've never loved a woman before you, and I hope that you'll realize that our love—yes, our love—will be able to deal with anything. Together. You know how to reach me when you do."

He then turned and left.

Chapter 17

By noon on Saturday, Rachel was ready to have a stiff drink. The entire bottle, if necessary. Her phone hadn't stopped ringing. Some calls she had answered and some she had not.

Ethan's calls were some of the ones she had not.

It seemed everyone was shocked by the tabloid's allegations that she'd been having a secret affair with Ethan, but they were happy if she had. Uncle Jacob and Aunt Lily told her not to be bothered by the accusations. Sofia inquired as to how she was holding up but didn't ask any specifics about the affair. So far no one believed the tabloid's headline that she only got involved with Ethan to further her career. That was so far from the truth. She had already had an up-and-coming career before Ethan appeared on the scene. But the goal of the tabloids was to sell papers, and with those kinds of accusations and the photos of them kissing in the studio lot, they created the sensationalism they craved.

Thanks to Charlene, who'd shown up for breakfast with a copy of *The Wagging Tongue* in her hand, she'd been forced to see the article. She wished she could claim the picture plastered on the front page had been doctored, but it hadn't.

Evidently, Paige had been around that night Ethan had shown up in the trailer unexpectedly. After they'd made love, he had walked her to her parked car. Since it was late, they assumed everyone had left and, before getting in her car, Ethan had pulled her into his arms and given her a very heated kiss. What she considered a special moment between them had been reduced to something sleazy, thanks to Paige and her cell phone camera.

She looked up from the book she'd been trying unsuccessfully to read when her house phone rang. She hoped the caller wasn't Ethan again. She couldn't help but smile when she heard the voice of Carmen Aiken on her answering machine.

"Rachel, I know you're there, so pick up this phone!"

Carmen was an Oscar-winning actress who was married to director/producer Matthew Birmingham. She and Carmen had become good friends when Carmen, new to Hollywood at the time, had been cast in one of

Matt's movies. Rachel had been the makeup artist on the set.

She reached for the phone and answered, "Okay, so you knew I was here."

"You've been holding back on me, girl. Ethan Chambers! Why did you keep that hunk a secret?"

Rachel wished it had been a secret she could have shared, but the only people who'd known about her affair with Ethan had been Charlene and Livia. "You know why, Carmen."

"Yes, I know how brutal the tabloids can be. Remember, I was a victim of their gossip for a while. Even after Matt and I remarried, they claimed we did it as a way to get publicity for his next movie."

Rachel was aware of that lie. Carmen and Matt had been divorced for a little over a year and had remarried last month. Rachel was glad they had worked out their differences and had gotten back together. She didn't know of any couple who deserved each other more.

"It really doesn't matter what those reporters think. It's how you feel, Rachel. I can tell from the photo that was one hell of a kiss he gave you. You're probably the envy of a lot of women today."

Rachel drew in a deep breath. Charlene had said the same thing, but it really didn't matter. She wanted no part of the tabloids and no part of Ethan.

She couldn't help but remember what he'd said before leaving and in the messages he'd left on her answering machine and cell. He said he loved her.

Well, she loved him, too, but in this case love would not be enough.

Carmen breached her silence. "I don't want you to make the same mistake I made, Rachel, by letting the tabloids rule your life."

Moments later when Rachel ended her call with Carmen, she knew it was too late. The tabloids were already ruling her life.

"What do you want, Curtis?"

"I like the publicity, Ethan, but you could have hooked up with another woman. It would have benefited your career a lot more had she been a model or an actress. She's a makeup artist, for crying out loud, regardless of the fact her last name is Wellesley."

An angry Ethan slouched back against the sofa with a beer bottle in one hand and his cell phone in the other. He didn't give a royal damn whether Curtis liked the publicity or not. That last comment alone meant the man's days as his agent were numbered.

When Ethan didn't say anything, Curtis continued, "Now what we need to do is to play our cards right with this publicity and keep it moving. But you need to get rid of the broad in that picture and get someone more newsworthy. Someone like Rayon Stewart. We can work the angle that Rachel Wellesley was just someone you were sleeping with while waiting for Rayon Stewart to end things with Artis Lomax."

"Go to hell, Curtis."

"Excuse me?"

"I said, go to hell. By the way, as of now, you're no longer my agent. You're fired."

He then hung up the phone and took a swig of his beer. He refused to let anyone put Rachel down. She was the best thing to ever happen to him, and he loved *her* and not some model or Hollywood actress.

He reached for his cell phone and punched in her number. He knew she was at her condo hiding out. He'd tried calling her all day but she refused to take any of his calls.

Joe Connors had been right. The article hadn't been pretty and had made Rachel look like a schemer who had used their affair to build her career. No doubt that was the story Paige had told the tabloids and they had run with it. If anyone would have bothered to check, they would have known it was all lies fabricated by a jealous woman.

When Rachel didn't answer, Ethan clicked off the phone before standing and moving to the window. The paparazzi was out there and had been all day, waiting for him to come out with a story. Well, he didn't have one. At the moment, the only thing he had was heartache.

Rachel braced herself for work Monday, knowing everyone had probably seen the tabloid's article. She had decided the best thing to do was to deal with it and move on. She had worked too hard to build her career to do otherwise.

Ethan had continued to call her through late last night and had called her again this morning. By her not answering his calls, she hoped he now realized she hadn't changed her mind. Ending things between them had been the best thing to do. It was important that anyone expecting drama would get the professional she had always been.

She appreciated that the studio lot was private. But that didn't stop the paparazzi from being crowded out front with their cameras ready to get a shot of her when she arrived at work. A few even tried blocking her car from going through the gate.

From the way everything got quiet when she walked onto the set, it was obvious she had been the topic of conversation. She gave everyone her cheery hello as usual while heading toward the trailer, but she didn't miss Paige's comment, which was intentionally loud enough for anyone to hear. "And she actually thought someone like Ethan Chambers could be interested in *her?*"

Rachel refused to turn and comment, but she couldn't help the smile when she heard Livia speak up. "Evidently he was interested in her, since she's the one with him in that photo, Paige."

Livia's words had no doubt hit a nerve with Paige, since everyone on set had seen her flirting outrageously with Ethan. Tae'Shawna had been just as bad. Some people on set had placed bets on which of the two— Paige or Tae'Shawna—would finally get his attention. Neither had.

Rachel kept walking to her trailer, intent on not being around when Ethan arrived. It would be bad enough having to work with him on the set knowing they would be the subject of everyone's attention. She needed to get herself together before seeing him.

She appreciated her two assistants giving their support with words of encouragement and letting her know if she and Ethan were an item, that meant he had good taste.

For the next hour or so she went about her day as usual, and when it was time for her to go out on the set she left her trailer. The last thing she wanted was to give the impression she was hiding out.

Ethan and Livia were in the middle of a scene where Dr. Duncan was explaining to Dr. Perry why they couldn't be together and why they needed to end things. Boy, that sounded familiar.

Several people turned to look at her, including Frasier and John, who both gave her nods. If they believed the tabloid story, then they knew she and Ethan had broken the show's rule. In which case, she knew her job was in jeopardy. If they had to choose which of them to keep, no doubt Ethan would stay, since he was their star.

"Freeze! Rachel, kill that shine on Ethan."

At Frasier's command, she moved forward. The set got quiet and she knew everyone was looking at her. At them. She greeted him only with his name when she stopped in front of him.

He did the same.

Their greeting sounded stiff. Being the professional she was, Rachel was determined to do her job. She took her makeup brush and swept across the bridge of his nose. She tried to ignore his scent, something she'd gotten used to, and the sound of his heavy breathing.

But she couldn't ignore the blue-gray eyes that seemed to watch her every moment. Emotions stirred within Rachel but she fought hard to keep them at bay. Making sure she didn't take any more time than necessary, she gave him a smile and said, "All done." And then she quickly walked away.

"Unfreeze!"

They resumed shooting the scene, and when she glanced over at Paige, there was a malicious smirk on the woman's face. Paige doubtless assumed it was Ethan who ended things between them and not the other way around. She was probably also thinking that although she might not be his date at the wrap party, neither would Rachel.

She didn't want to be the object of discussion and speculation. But since she was, she would do everything she could to stay professional and put her and Ethan's affair behind her.

No matter how much it hurt.

"Ethan, wait up."

He glanced around and saw Tae'Shawna approach with a smile on her face. Out of the corner of his eye, he saw Paige watching. She'd had the good sense to avoid him today.

"What is it, Tae'Shawna?"

"I see you're scheduled for makeup with Rachel tomorrow."

"And what of it?"

"If you're uncomfortable about it, I'll speak to John for you to have one of her assistants do it."

He didn't need Tae'Shawna to tell him of his schedule. He knew Rachel would be doing his makeup, which meant they would be alone in the trailer for a short while. But he figured to keep talk down, Rachel had already arranged for one of her assistants either to do his makeup or be there with her when she did it. He doubted very seriously they would be alone.

He looked at Tae'Shawna. "Why would I be uncomfortable with Rachel doing my makeup?"

She shrugged. "I just assumed since the news is out about how she came on to you to boost her career that you are leery of her now. Coming on to you was unprofessional on her part."

Ethan put his hands in the pockets of his jeans and he didn't care one iota about the fierce frown that settled on his face. He was sick and tired of people assuming the worst of Rachel. Bottom line was he had pursued her, he had wanted her. He still wanted her.

"First of all," he told Tae'Shawna, "anyone with good sense knows most of what's printed in those tabloids isn't true. Second of all, Rachel is one of the most professional women I know. She didn't have to come on to me because I found her attractive from day one. I saw in her something I haven't seen in a lot of woman lately."

Tae'Shawna lifted her chin and he could tell his words had hit a nerve. "And what is that?"

"Unselfishness. She is not self-absorbed and I doubt that she has a shallow bone in her body. In fact, she never came on to me, but *you* did, many times, right here on the set. So who should I think is the professional one? Now if you'll excuse me, I need to call it a day."

A few hours later, in the privacy of his home, Ethan sank down on his sofa frustrated as hell. He hadn't tried making any type of contact with Rachel while on the set but he had called her several times since getting home, and she still would not accept his calls. If the paparazzi were on her tail like they were on his, he could imagine what she was going through, but that was no reason to block him out of her life.

Considering everything, he had expected her to withdraw for a day or so, but he hadn't expected her to put up an emotional wall that he could not penetrate.

For the last three days on the set she had been cordial yet distant, as if to prove to everyone that they were not together. When she looked at him, it was as if she was looking straight through him. He knew she was trying hard to maintain a mask of nonchalance where he was concerned, determined to avoid any situation that would compromise her professionalism.

He had tried not to be angered by her actions but a part of him couldn't help it. And now in the comfort of his home, lonely as it was, his anger was turning into intense hurt.

Why was he letting her do this to him?

Because, as he had told her, he loved her and a part of him believed she loved him back. And he believed that one day she would realize that nothing, not the paparazzi and not the threat of jeopardizing her career, was worth sacrificing their love.

Rachel cuddled on her sofa and pressed the replay button to pick up her last call.

"Rachel, this is Ethan. I know what you're going through but I wish you would let us go through it together. When you hurt, I hurt. I love you and I know you love me. Baby, please don't do this to us."

She glanced over at the beautiful bouquet of flowers that had been delivered to her from Ethan by way of Charlene. Her best friend had dropped by with the flowers earlier that evening. The card attached simply said:

I love you.
Ethan

Tears rolled from her eyes. She didn't think it would be so hard giving him up. She hadn't counted on the agony and the pain, the feeling of loneliness and heartbreak. It was hard during the day to see him and try to ignore him. Alone in her trailer, she would feel alienated. Even after three days, everyone on the set was still abuzz about her and Ethan breaking the rules, but so far neither Frasier nor John had approached her or Ethan. She figured they were probably waiting for one of them to approach them first, so tomorrow she would.

Tomorrow... Tomorrow she was scheduled to do Ethan's makeup. Typically they would be alone in her trailer, but she didn't want everyone speculating about what they were doing or saying behind closed doors. To have one of her assistants fill in for her would indicate she wasn't professional enough to handle a controversial situation. So in a way it was a "damned if you do and damned if you don't" situation.

Livia had come to her rescue. She volunteered to be the buffer by being in the trailer at the same time Ethan was there, on the pretext of repairing a broken nail or something. Rachel hoped the ploy worked.

Ethan knew all eyes were on him as he headed for Rachel's trailer. No doubt there were some who had their watch set to see how long he stayed inside alone with her.

"Ethan, wait up." He stopped and glanced around. Livia was walking toward him. She was one of the few women on set who hadn't tried coming on to him. Like Rachel, she was a specialist in her craft. Even with all those love scenes they'd done, they had still maintained professionalism.

"I need to see Rachel a minute myself," she said, smiling. "Broken nail."

He smiled, seeing through her ploy. Rachel was her friend and she was making an attempt to avoid gossip and speculation.

From the look on Rachel's face when they entered her trailer, Ethan knew for certain that Livia's appearance had been planned. Rachel showed no surprise at seeing them both walk in.

"Hello, Ethan, you can take my chair. And Livia, I'll fix that nail in a minute, just as soon as I finish with Ethan."

"No problem," Livia said, smiling. "I'll just sit over here."

"You can go ahead and take care of Livia and then do me," Ethan suggested. Only after the words had left his mouth did he realize their double meaning.

"No, Livia can wait until I finish with you," Rachel insisted.

"And I don't have a problem with you doing her first."

Before Rachel could open her mouth to retort, Livia spoke up. "Look, guys, evidently you two need time alone to clear up a few things."

"No, we don't."

"Yes, we do."

Livia shook her head. "Since the two of you can't agree, I'll make the decision for you," she said. "Rachel, you can work on Ethan while I excuse myself a minute to go to the ladies' room." Livia then headed toward the back of the trailer where the dressing room and bathroom were located.

Rachel watched her friend's retreating back.

"You can take care of me now, Rachel."

Rachel turned and glared at Ethan. "Do you not care about my career?"

His face rigid, he returned her glare. "And do you not care about my heart? Or yours?"

Her stomach twisted with his question, and she forced

herself to ignore the stab of pain that ripped through her. "I care, but there's nothing I can do about it, Ethan. Please just let me make you up so I can be ready for the next person."

"Fine, get to it then."

He reclined in the chair and she stood over him. She hesitated a moment and looked into the eyes staring back at her. Just like always when she looked at them, she was in awe of their beauty, but this time she saw the anger and pain in their depths.

Drawing in a deep breath, she brushed foundation across his cheekbones, then around his mouth, and she couldn't help but focus on his lips. Lips she had kissed so many times. Lips she wanted to kiss again. But she fought doing so.

Those lips moved and she heard the husky but low tone of his voice. "I love you, Rachel."

She dropped the brush from her hand and took a step back. "I'm finished, Ethan."

He eased out of the chair, his long legs bringing him to stand directly in front of her. "You might be finished but I'm not, Rachel. At least not where you're concerned. What we've shared is too precious and I won't give up on us. Admit that you love me as much as I love you."

She looked up at him, her heart full, but was unable to say the words he wanted to hear. "Ethan, I—I can't say it."

He reached out and gently pulled her into his arms and she could not have pulled out of them even if she wanted to. He lowered his head and, of their own accord, her lips parted as she sighed his name. The moment his lips touched hers she felt soothed by something she had missed for the past couple of days, something her body had gotten used to having.

A sensuous shudder passed through her as his tongue reinstated its rights to her mouth, letting her know that no matter how she continued to deny them, put distance between them, there would always be this—a passion so intense and forceful, it would take more than negative publicity to destroy it.

When he angled his head to deepen the kiss, she stretched up on tiptoes to get the full Ethan Chambers effect. And it was worth every effort. He was kissing her like a starving man, and in kind, she was kissing him like a starving woman. Her heart swelled with every stroke of his tongue, and she knew in her heart what she refused to speak out loud.

He finally pulled his mouth away and tenderly touched her cheek. "One day you will tell me that you love me and I'll be ready to hear it when you do." His tone was raw and husky and sent sensuous shivers all down her spine.

He leaned down and brushed a kiss across her lips before turning to walk out of the trailer.

Chapter 18

Rachel's lips twitched in a smile when the limousine pulled up behind Amaury's, an exclusive restaurant in Hollywood whose doors usually were closed until eight every night. Only Sofia, with a list of connections and contacts a mile long, could make the impossible happen.

For the past week, other than leaving for work, Rachel had pretty much stayed in and not ventured out with the paparazzi breathing down her neck. Although the breakup between Rayon Stewart and Artis Lomax and rumors of another adoption by Brad and Angelina now dominated the headlines, there were a few reporters who just didn't know when to quit.

"We're here, Ms. Rachel."

"Thanks, Martin," she said to the man who'd been the limo driver for Limelight Entertainment for years. She could recall sitting in the backseat of the huge car, with him behind the wheel, while being transported to and from private school as a child of no more than eight or nine. During those days, he kept her entertained with his own rendition of the animated voices of Bugs Bunny and Daffy Duck. He used to be so good at it.

Moments later, he was holding the door open for her as she got out. Amaury Gaston met her at the door and gave her a big hug.

"Sofia is already seated and waiting on you, Rachel," he said in a heavy French accent.

"Thanks."

"I've prepared your favorite," he added.

Rachel licked her lips. Chicken cordon bleu, she guessed, and Amaury's was the best. "You like spoiling me and Sofia," she said, smiling.

"Yes, just like I used to enjoy spoiling your parents. They were two of my first customers, and your father proposed to your mother right here one night. It was very special."

Rachel had heard the story before but didn't mind hearing it again. According to everyone who knew them, her parents had been very much in love.

"And I know if they were alive, they would want me to treat their girls just as special as I thought they were," Amaury added.

Moments later, Rachel made her way toward the table where her sister sat waiting. Sofia saw her approach and smiled. With her beauty and tall, slender figure, Rachel thought Sofia could have easily been a model or actress. Instead, she had followed in their father's footsteps and had taken his place in the family business working alongside Uncle Jacob. Despite their age difference, she and Sofia had maintained a close relationship, especially now that Sofia wasn't as overprotective as she used to be.

Sofia stood and Rachel walked straight into her sister's outstretched arms. Then Sofia took a step back and studied her from head to toe. "Hmm, it doesn't look like the tabloids have beaten you up too badly, although I'm sure there are scars on the inside that I can't see."

Rachel felt a thickness in her throat. She hadn't intended to let Sofia know just how shaken up she really was. Ethan's kiss yesterday had done that enough. She had expected him to call last night, but he hadn't. She wasn't sure what she would have said if he had.

"Are you okay, Rach?" Sofia asked, looking into her eyes.

"Yes."

"You sure?"

Rachel forced a smile. "Yes, I'm fine. Come on, let's let Amaury know we're ready to be served. I'm starving," she said, moving to her chair and away from her sister's intense scrutiny.

"Okay, but don't think you're not going to tell me everything," Sofia said, taking her own seat again.

"Everything like what?"

Sofia held her gaze with that "let's get serious"

expression on her face. "Everything like how you really feel about Ethan Chambers."

"Maybe we ought to buy stock in those tabloids since you seem to be in them quite a bit these days, Ethan."

Ethan closed his refrigerator after pulling out a cold beer. He juggled the phone as he twisted off the cap. His heart had begun pounding in his chest when the phone had rung, in hopes the caller was Rachel. Instead it was Hunter. "That's a possibility."

"So is any of it true?" his brother asked.

"The only thing I will admit to is an involvement with Rachel. Her motives were exploited falsely. Our being together was mutual and she didn't need me to advance her career. She did that on her own."

"Pretty defensive, aren't you?"

"Can't help but be where she's concerned. I love her."

There was silence on the other end, and Ethan was well aware that his brother was recovering from what he'd said. In all his twenty-eight years, he'd never admitted to loving any woman. While his brother was pondering what he'd said, Ethan took a swig of beer.

"This is serious," Hunter finally said.

"I hope she realizes that it is. She's tabloid shy."

"And you're just the opposite," Hunter pointed out. "For as long as I can recall, you enjoyed getting in front of a camera."

Ethan shrugged, remembering some of his wild

escapades while in high school and college. "Not when they portray my woman in a bad light."

"Well, we're all looking forward to meeting her. And since things are that serious, don't forget the traditional Chambers vineyard weddings."

Ethan smiled. "I won't, but first I have to convince her that she loves me and that I will make her life with me worth anything the tabloids might put her through."

"Good luck."

Ethan drew in a deep breath. "Thanks." He knew he was going to need it.

Sofia took another sip of her wine. "And you think Livia Blake might be looking for another agent?" she asked.

"Yes," Rachel said, eager to keep her sister talking about something else other than her and Ethan. "Livia says at thirty her modeling days are coming to an end, and she wants an agent who will take her acting career to another level and run with it. Of course, she's heard about Limelight Entertainment and would love to talk to you, but she's heard how selective you are."

Sofia didn't deny what Rachel said. She *was* selective. "I've been keeping an eye on Livia Blake's modeling career for a while now and wondered if she planned on doing anything beyond that. Limelight is definitely interested, so have her give me a call."

Rachel looked at her sister and could tell she was bothered about something and that it was something other than what was going on with her and Ethan.

"You've been working a lot lately, Sofia. When do you plan on taking another vacation?"

Sofia smiled. "Hmm, a vacation sounds nice but I won't be going back to the islands any time soon. My clientele has doubled, and I have to find work for a lot of people." She took another sip of her wine, leaned back in her chair and asked, "Did you know Uncle Jacob is thinking about retiring?"

Rachel's eyes widened. "No. I talked to him a few days ago and he said nothing about that. But I can see him wanting to just chill, take it easy and travel. He and Aunt Lily have been saying they want to build that house in Barbados for years."

"Yes, I'd love for him to retire and enjoy life, too, but not if the rumors I'm hearing are true."

Rachel lifted a brow. "What rumors?"

Although there weren't others in the restaurant, Sofia leaned over the table and said in a low tone, "I've heard that he's thinking about selling his interest in Limelight to Ramell Jordan at A.F.I."

Rachel's expression denoted her surprise. Artists Factory Inc. had been a rival talent agency of Limelight Entertainment for years. In fact, Ramell's father, Emmett, had been a close friend of her father's, but for some reason they were not on good terms at the time of her dad's death. And because of Sofia's close relationship with their father, Rachel was not surprised that her sister would not favor a possible merger.

"What you heard is probably just a rumor," Rachel

said, hoping that would smooth her sister's ruffled feathers.

"I certainly hope so. I can't believe Uncle Jacob would consider doing such a thing."

Rachel could see why he would. Although her father and Emmett Jordan had ended on bad terms, Uncle Jacob and Emmett had remained somewhat friendly.

"Ramell Jordan is nothing more than the son of a backstabber after what Emmett did to Dad," Sofia said angrily.

Rachel lifted a brow. "And just what did he do to Dad?"

She'd always believed there was more to the story than either she or Sofia knew, but no one would ever say. In fact, Sofia was the only one who'd ever made such accusations about Emmett Jordan. All Uncle Jacob would say was that it had been a misunderstanding between the two men and that had her father lived, his and Emmett's relationship would have been restored to a close friendship.

"You're better off not knowing."

Rachel only shook her head. For years that had been the same response Sofia gave her whenever she asked. Maybe she was simply better off not knowing.

"And now that you've tried to get me to avoid talking about you and Ethan Chambers, I think that we need to finally get to the meat of your problem."

Rachel pushed away her plate. Dinner had been delicious and now she was ready for desert and coffee.

But she would wait awhile until after she answered the questions she knew her sister had for her.

"There's really nothing to tell, Sofia. You know how I detest being in the public eye and Ethan's popularity right now puts him there, as well as any woman he's involved with."

"So the two of you *are* involved?"

Pain rolled through Rachel. "We *were* involved."

Sofia studied her sister's features, saw the pain that settled in her face. "The two of you kept things between you a secret from everyone—including me—which evidently was working for a while. So what happened?"

Rachel took a deep breath, and then she told Sofia about what Paige had done.

A deep frown appeared on Sofia's face. "And this Paige person works on the set of *Paging the Doctor?*"

"Yes, she's a production assistant."

"Not for long," Sofia muttered under her breath. "Tell me something, Rachel. Did your affair with Ethan have substance or was it all about sex?"

Rachel met her sister's inquisitive gaze. It would be so easy to claim it had been nothing but sex, but this was Sofia and she'd always had a way of seeing through any lie Rachel told. Besides, she would tell Sofia what she hadn't told anyone, not even Ethan.

"I love him, Sofia. It wasn't all about sex."

Her sister stared at her for a long moment, and then a smile touched her lips when she said, "Then I can see no reason why the two of you can't be together."

Rachel rolled her eyes. In a way she was surprised at her sister's comment, since Sofia of all people knew how she guarded her privacy. "You know that's not possible, Sofia. Ethan is an up-and-coming star, and being the focus of a lot of attention is what will boost his career. I can't risk that kind of publicity with the career I tried so hard to build."

"And what else?"

Rachel gave her sister a confused look. "What do you mean what else?"

Sofia leaned in closer. "This is me, and I can read you like a book, Rachel. So level with me and tell me the real reason you and Ethan can't be together. Since I'm always on the lookout for potential clients, I'm well aware that Ethan Chambers is hot news. I'm also well aware that during the time the two of you were having your secret tryst, his name wasn't linked to any Hollywood starlet, which made the tabloids wonder exactly what he was doing and who he was doing it with. And when it seemed he had decided to just live a boring life, they backed off. When the news hit the papers about the two of you, the tabloids had basically given him a rest."

Sofia paused to take a sip of her wine and then asked, "And what's this I hear about you taking a temporary leave from the show?"

Rachel placed her wine glass down after taking her own sip. She didn't have to wonder where Sofia had gotten the news. Few people knew that Frasier considered himself as their godfather. "I thought it would be best, and I met with Frasier yesterday. He wasn't all that keen on the idea but said since there was only a week left for filming, he would go along with it. But he wanted me back on my job when they began the new season. I can handle that."

Sofia lifted a brow. "Can you? They aren't writing Ethan out of the script, so he'll be returning, too. Will you be able to handle that?"

"I don't have a choice."

"Yes, you do. For once you can fight for what you want, what you have every right to have."

Rachel was still surprised by her sister's attitude. She'd expected her to be the voice of reason and agree with her that the best thing was to put her career ahead of anything else. That was certainly what Sofia was doing these days. She couldn't recall a time when her sister had gotten serious about a man.

"You don't think my career is important, Sofia?"

Sofia waved off her words. "Of course I do, but your heart takes priority."

At Rachel's frown, Sofia reached out and captured her hand in hers. "Hear me out for a second, Rach." She paused and then said, "This is the first time I can truly say I believe you're in love. It shows on your face every time you say Ethan's name. You, little sister, are truly in love and I don't believe it's one-sided. I've been waiting to see how Ethan was going to respond to the tabloids. He hasn't denied the two of you are having an affair. In fact, he's gone on record with Joe Connors to say that you were not using him to boost your career. Other than that, he's been low-key about everything, which shows me he's doing whatever he can to protect you, and I like him for that. He could take all this publicity and run with it, but he hasn't. He's trying to fade to black."

Rachel had to agree with Sofia on that. Ethan was keeping a low profile these days.

"A man like that is worth keeping, Rach. And it's time you do what I haven't been able to do yet."

"And what is that?" Rachel asked, taking another sip of her wine.

"Stop hiding behind your career as an excuse to avoid falling in love. It's an unfortunate Wellesley trait. I'm guilty of it, too. We're both scared that if we love someone, they will abandon us like Mom and Dad did."

Rachel met her sister's gaze. Is that what she had been doing? Was that the reason she'd deliberately kept men at arm's length? Although she was barely out of diapers when her parents were killed, and her uncle and aunt had always been there for her, she had grown up feeling a tremendous loss. It had been hard during her early years when all her friends had had someone to call Mom and she had not. A part of her had always had that inner fear that to love also meant to lose. Wasn't it time for her to finally take a chance on love and believe she was deserving of a forever kind of love like everyone else? Did she want to live the rest of her life afraid of the unknown? Wasn't a life with Ethan better than a life without him? In her heart she knew that it was, and it was time for her to take a leap of faith and take control of her life.

A smile touched Rachel's face when she recalled the party planned for the cast and crew this weekend. "You're right. It's time for me to stop hiding."

Chapter 19

"You look simply beautiful, Rach," Charlene said, smiling as she gazed at her best friend from head to toe.

"And I feel beautiful," Rachel responded, looking at herself in a full-length mirror. She glanced over her shoulder at the woman who was smiling proudly at her handiwork. "Livia, I'm thinking that maybe I ought to be worried. You could take my job as a makeup artist."

Livia chuckled as she waved off her words. "You don't have to worry about that, and thanks to your sister I won't either. I appreciate you putting in a good word for me. It's a dream come true to be represented by Limelight Entertainment."

Rachel smiled as she looked at herself in the mirror

again. Sofia had gone shopping with her and helped her pick out her dress, Charlene had selected the accessories and Livia had done her makeup and hair. She felt like Cinderella about to go to the most important ball of her life. And her Prince Charming was waiting.

At least she hoped he was waiting.

She'd heard from Livia that Ethan had gone home to Napa Valley last weekend and that on the set for the season finale he had thrown himself into his work and pretty much kept to himself. More than once she was tempted to call him but decided to do things this way. Now nerves were setting in and all those "what-ifs" were stirring through her mind.

She turned to her two friends. "Are you sure he's coming to the wrap party tonight, Livia?"

Livia smiled. "I heard him assure Frasier that he'll be there to walk the red carpet."

Rachel nodded. "What if he brings a date?"

"I doubt that, and I even heard him tell Frasier that he's coming alone," Livia responded. "And just so you know, Paige was dropped from the show. All I know is that she got called to John's office and he told her she was no longer needed. So the only thing she gained by stirring up that mess with the tabloids is an unemployment check." Livia smiled and added, "And I heard she's having trouble finding a job. Seems like someone put the word out around town about her."

Rachel didn't have to guess who. Her sister was that influential.

"I think it's time for you to leave now," Charlene said, glancing out the window. "Martin just pulled up."

Nervous flutters raced through Rachel's stomach. Sofia had called her from London, where she'd gone to meet with a client, and given her another pep talk. Then Uncle Jacob and Aunt Lily had called and told her to follow her heart, and since they would be at the wrap party, they would see her later.

Rachel knew she was doing the right thing. Ethan had said he wanted her to tell him that she loved him and she was prepared to do that. And it no longer mattered who would be listening. She did love him, and she needed him in her life more than anything. It was about time that he knew it.

Ethan drew in a deep breath when the limo he was riding in alone pulled to a stop in front of the red carpet. The crowd was massive and, as usual, reporters were out in droves. People were standing behind the roped areas, and cameras were flashing from just about every angle.

More than anything, he wished Rachel would have been there with him, by his side, to bask in the moment of his accomplishments. He had worked hard to reach this point in his career and, more than anything, he wanted the woman he loved to be with him.

He had told her that he loved her and now the next step would have to be hers. And he could only hope that sooner or later she'd make it.

He had to believe that one day she would realize

that together their love was strong enough to withstand anything. Even this, he thought, glancing out the car window at the crowd that seemed to be getting larger by the minute.

As soon as he stepped out of the car, flashbulbs went off, momentarily blinding him, and he was immediately pulled center stage to be interviewed. The cheering crowd made him feel good, but nothing could heal his broken heart.

"Everyone, we have Ethan Chambers, who this season became known as Dr. Tyrell Perry on *Paging the Doctor.* And how are you doing tonight, Ethan?"

Ethan smiled for the camera while giving his attention to the red-carpet host for the evening, Neill Carter. "I'm doing great, Neill, and looking forward to a wonderful evening."

Neill laughed. "I can believe that, but you came by yourself, man. Surely there was a special lady who would have loved to make this walk down the red carpet with you."

It was Saturday night and, more than likely, millions of people were sitting in front of their television sets watching the festivities, including his family. He hoped Rachel was one of those watching because he intended to give her a shout-out. Even if no one else knew whom his message was meant for, she would.

"Yes," he said, looking directly into the camera. "There is a special lady for me and I want her to know that I…"

He stopped talking when he glanced over Neill's

shoulder and saw a woman strolling toward them. He blinked. She was beautiful, from the way her hair was styled on her head to the gorgeous red gown she wore—down to the silver shoes that sparkled on her feet.

His gaze returned to her face and for a moment he didn't believe what he was seeing. Rachel was here, in the spotlight, and it was obvious she wasn't there to make anyone up behind the scenes tonight. She was standing out and she was walking toward him.

All eyes were on her, including his. When she reached his side, she smiled and leaned closer and whispered in his ear, "I love you, Ethan. Thanks for waiting on me."

He couldn't help the smile that touched his lips. He had waited on her. And that wait had not been in vain. He pulled her into his arms and lowered his mouth to hers, kissing her right there in front of everyone. It was a move that caused the crowd to roar with excitement. Photographers snapped pictures, taking it all in. When Ethan finally released Rachel's mouth, he grinned down at her as flashes continued to go off around them.

"I take it you two know each other," Neill said with a teasing grin.

"Yes, we know each other," Ethan said, pulling her closer to his side. "This is my special lady, and she has something I've never given another female."

"And what's that?" Neill asked.

"My heart."

Later that night, Ethan opened the door to *their* place and swept Rachel into his arms. The party had been great. He'd made more contacts and had gotten numerous offers from new agents looking to fill Curtis Fairgate's place.

But the highlight of the entire evening was the woman in his arms, the star of his heart.

He tried to maintain control as he carried her to the bed. His hands began shaking as he slowly undressed her, hoping and praying this wasn't a dream and he wouldn't wake up to an empty room.

It was only after he'd gotten them both undressed and eased on the bed with her, right into her outstretched arms, that he finally accepted this was the real deal. He took her face in his hands and stared into the darkness of her eyes as his heart swelled even more. "I love you, Rachel."

Her smile brightened his whole world, and her voice was filled with sincerity when she said, "And I love you, Ethan."

For a suspended moment in time they stared at each other, and then he captured her lips with his as joy bubbled within him. He knew at that moment that he'd been made to love her, to be her shelter from the storm, to protect her, to honor her for always.

He deepened the kiss and felt her body tremble. When he settled his body over hers, he knew he was almost home.

He had wanted to take things slow with her, but it had been too long since they'd been together like this and his body was craving to get inside of her. When she moaned his name he knew he couldn't wait any longer.

He broke off the kiss to gaze down into her eyes at the same time he thrust inside of her, entering her with a hunger that shook every part of his body. As her scent swept through his nostrils and her inner muscles gripped him for everything they could get, he threw his head back and surrendered to her.

"Rachel!"

His sexy pixie was making her mark, and each time she lifted her hips to meet his thrusts, stroke for stroke, he was pushed even more over the edge. When he felt a mind-blowing explosion on the horizon, he glanced back down into her face and saw his passion mirrored in her eyes.

When the climax hit, he could swear bells and whistles went off. Their bodies exploded together, escalating them to the stars and beyond. They shuddered together as the power of love drenched them in an orgasm so potent he wondered if they would ever be able to recover.

But deep down he knew they would—only to take the journey over and over again, for an entire lifetime.

When their bodies ceased shuddering, he rolled to the side, pulled her into his arms and held her close to his heart. Just where she would always be.

Rachel lay contented in Ethan's arms. She hadn't realized how much she'd missed coming here, being here with him, until they'd stopped being together. But never again.

They had made love several times, and she kept

telling him how much she loved him because she loved hearing herself say it and he seemed to enjoy hearing it. And he told her how much he loved her as well. She knew now that together they could face anything. She was no longer afraid of what the tabloids might print or how her career could be affected.

Tonight Frasier had congratulated everyone and indicated that he expected them all back for the new season. Everyone except Paige, of course, who ironically wasn't invited to the wrap party she'd been dying to attend with Ethan. And Tae'Shawna Miller. Apparently she had whined one time too many, because rumor had it she'd been released from the show as well.

Rachel shifted her body to glance up at Ethan. "You're quiet. What are you thinking?" she asked him.

He smiled down at her. "I was thinking about how surprised I was to see you tonight. Surprised and happy. What made you come?"

She reached up and her fingers touched his cheek. "You. I knew I loved you and you kept telling me that you loved me, breaking down my barriers." She paused a moment and then said, "And I also realized Sofia was right. I was hiding my love on the pretense of protecting my career when I was really afraid to admit loving you. I was afraid I wouldn't be able to handle it if you were to leave me the way my parents did."

Ethan held her gaze. "I'll never leave you, sweetheart. And by the way, while you were talking to Frasier tonight, I got a call on my cell phone. It was my mother. She was watching the whole thing on television and heard me when I said you had my heart. So she wants to know when's the wedding."

Rachel laughed. "The wedding?"

"Yes. I told her I hadn't gotten around to asking you yet." He pulled her closer into his arms. "So, baby, will you marry me?"

She smiled up at him. "For better or for worse?"

He nodded. "And richer or poorer."

"In sickness and in health?"

He chuckled. "Until death do us part."

She leaned up and threw her arms around his neck. "In that case, I accept!"

He wrapped her in his arms and kissed her, sealing what he knew would be a Hollywood marriage that would last forever.

* * * * *

L♥VE IN THE LIMELIGHT
Fantasy, Fame and Fortune...Hollywood-Style!

Book #1
By *New York Times* and *USA TODAY*
Bestselling Author Brenda Jackson

STAR OF HIS HEART
August 2010

Book #2
By A.C. Arthur

SING YOUR PLEASURE
September 2010

Book #3
By Ann Christopher

SEDUCED ON THE RED CARPET
October 2010

Book #4
By *Essence* Bestselling Author Adrianne Byrd

LOVERS PREMIERE
November 2010

*Set in Hollywood's entertainment industry,
two unstoppable sisters and their two friends
find romance, glamour and dreams-come-true.*

*Melanie Harte's exclusive matchmaking service—
the Platinum Society—can help any soul find
their ideal mate. Because when love is perfect,
it is a match made in heaven.*

ESSENCE BESTSELLING AUTHOR

DONNA HILL

Melanie Harte's reputation as a
matchmaker depends on her
"never get involved with a client"
rule. Yet she soon finds herself
pursued by both Rafe Lawson
and Claude Montgomery. Both
men are incredibly sexy—and
definitely off-limits. But as
Melanie's feelings intensify,
keeping her company's good
name means risking her own
perfect match.

**"THROUGH THE FIRE is a
deeply emotional romance
with characters who are
literally fighting to bring
living back into their lives."**
—*RT Book Reviews*

HEART'S REWARD
A Match Made Novel

*Coming July 27, 2010,
wherever books are sold.*

www.kimanipress.com
www.myspace.com/kimanipress

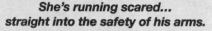

REQUEST YOUR FREE BOOKS!

2 FREE NOVELS
PLUS 2 FREE GIFTS!

KIMANI™
ROMANCE

Love's ultimate destination!